LOVE AND DECEPTION

SASKIA WOODHILL

Lightpool Publishing

www.lightpoolpublishing.com

On a sunny Saturday in early spring, Amy stood deep in thought on the steps outside the Victoria and Albert Museum waiting for her friend Kate to arrive for their weekend coffee date. In her mind she still dwelled on what she had been writing that morning, so engrossed that she didn't notice Kate standing a couple of steps above her, studying her with a thoughtful look before she descended and touched Amy's shoulder.

'Helloooo!' she said loudly, and Amy jumped. 'God, you gave me a fright! I thought you weren't here yet.'

'I got here early – let's go inside. The place is filling up rapidly, I just had a look.'

With their coffees in front of them Amy stopped mid-sentence and watched amused as Kate took a bite out of her almond croissant then held it up and studied it with a frown as if she had no idea where it had come from. 'I don't know why I ordered this. I'm supposed to be on a diet, but I've got a weak mind, and I love these. And you didn't order anything to eat – you didn't last time either.'

Amy said seriously, 'Someone you trust probably told you to get it.'

'What on earth do you mean? Surely you didn't whisper evil ideas in my ear when we ordered?' She took another bite and sighed with pleasure. 'But now I have it, I'll enjoy it – one of the most satisfying things to eat ever invented.'

'Didn't you read about it on the BBC website the other day? It was on the science page, an article about neuroscience. They've found that some people eat things they know they shouldn't, because they hear this little voice in their head, the voice of someone they know and trust, their mother perhaps, or their best friend – their mind manufactures the voice. And the voice tells them it's ok to eat whatever it is they're trying to resist – just this once - and then they can go back to being sensible about losing weight. It's the trusted voice that does the trick, it makes you feel it's ok.' She shook her head in disbelief. 'Fancy your brain tricking you to do something bad! Amazing!'

For a brief moment Kate looked stunned then she burst out laughing. 'You know what? You *are* crazy. Melissa warned me to be careful after she introduced us. She said you often play tricks on people who would never suspect you'd do anything like it. Neuroscience! Ha!' She pointed the croissant at Amy. 'I've never met anyone with such a serious job, someone who looks so sane and sensible and *quiet*, if you don't mind me saying - and who's also totally bonkers.'

Amy reached out, took the croissant out of Kate's hand and looked closely at it before she took a small bite and handed it back. 'Nice, but too sweet.'

'You should be a novelist with that crazy imagination, you really should. And why didn't your little voice tell *you* to buy a croissant?'

'I lost my taste for sweet things when I had Covid the second time, and now I can't abide most cakes and things, but for some reason chocolate is ok. No, I'm not kidding this time, it's true - it took me completely by surprise. One day I still liked my shortbread biscuits and the next day I bit into one I was having with my coffee and just spat it out. The sweetness of it just felt revolting, so that bite I stole of yours was wasted. Sorry, but it was a good opportunity to test if it had changed. Not that I hanker after sweet things now, but I kind of miss them, strange thought that sounds and ...'

Her voice trailed off as a strong smell of overheated cooking oil swirled around her and she knew danger was close. "Oh damn! I can smell him – he's here somewhere.'

With Kate staring at her she turned slowly and scanned the room, then further around towards the entrance, and there he was. He had stopped to talk to someone, and his back was in their direction, but at any moment now he might turn around and spot her. Her ex-partner Simon.

'Oh no, please God, don't do this to me,' she pleaded quietly. 'Kate, I'll apologise in advance, but I think Simon is nearly bound to notice me at some stage and then he'll come over and make a nuisance of himself. You've never met him, of course - we broke up before I got to know you, but he confronted me a couple of weeks ago when I was out having a drink with some people from work, and it got very embarrassing.'

Kate studied her for a few moments with a look of concern, then she smiled, seemingly unfazed by this alarming prospect. 'And if he does, would you like me to get rid of him - like send him on his way really, really fast? Or would that be even more embarrassing?'

Inside Amy's head a little video clip of her short, slightly chubby friend trying to deal with Simon played out, and it didn't end well. She couldn't let Kate risk becoming another trembling victim of Simon's scorn, that master of withering sarcasm.

'Oh no, don't do that, *please* don't! He can very nasty - he gets rude and personal when he's riled or when he wants to punish someone. That handsome face and the sexy body are no indications of what's inside.' Amy spoke very quietly with her head half turned towards the pillar covered in glittering mosaic beside their table, as if she was admiring it or commenting on it. 'I've tried and failed to get him to leave me alone. He's got a thick hide and a huge sense of entitlement, and he's never forgiven me for being the one who broke it off. He thinks that should be his prerogative, so now he enjoys tormenting me in public whenever we happen to be in the same place.'

'You should check your phone. A few weeks ago, a friend of mine discovered that her husband had put a tracking app on her phone, so he could see where she went and even how long she was in each location. I asked what she did when she discovered, and she said she deleted the app and changed the PIN on her phone, and then a few days later she spotted him in the kitchen when he'd offered to tidy up after dinner, and he was trying to unlock her phone - and failing.'

'Did she confront him? Or leave him?'

'Oh, God no – she says she'll get her own back when it suits her, she's planning the retribution now. They have a crazy marriage, like they hate and love each other at the same time. Constant silent, devious battles being played out.'

To Amy this situation seemed bizarre. How could a woman, who was being treated like a possession, stay with a man like that? She took a sip of coffee and looked straight at Kate over the rim of the cup to avoid her eyes swivelling to see where Simon had sat down. She knew he was still there - the smell of over-heated oil was still hanging in the air and the urge to know exactly where he sat was nearly impossible to resist. And then it happened, just what she had feared. While Amy kept her gaze firmly fixed on Kate, Simon had spotted her, and suddenly he was standing right beside her with his hand reaching out as if he was about to put it on her shoulder, or worse, grip her around the back of the neck like he did in that bistro a fortnight ago. That pretend-affectionate but painful grip to dominate her.

She swivelled in her chair and looked up at him and tried to make her voice expressionless, desperately hoping she looked calm. 'Simon,' she said with no form of greeting and without a smile.

His hand was now suspended mid-air and when she said nothing else and just continued to look at him, he bent down as if to put his arm around her shoulders and said in the fake caressing voice he could put on at the drop of a hat, 'How are you, my treasure? I haven't seen you for a couple of weeks. We must get together soon for a drink or dinner.'

Suddenly Amy didn't care if there was a scene, but for once she had to draw a line in the sand even if public embarrassment followed. 'No Simon, we're *not* getting together for a drink or dinner - or for anything else for that matter. Our relationship was over long ago, so just *leave me alone*, please.'

She wasn't quite sure where the courage had come from to say this in that dismissive, firm tone of voice, but it was probably linked to the fact that Kate was sitting on the other side of the table, not some other friend, who had known Simon for years but couldn't see him for what he really was.

'Oh, you naughty wench, you do like teasing me, don't you?' Simon's voice was playful, but his eyes were hard and cold. 'I'll call you and make a date.

'I'll block your number.' She knew she was taking an ever increasing risk of retribution, because he had never been averse to raised voices and potential scenes in public. He thrived on attention of any kind, and her inner tension was rising by the second. But before Simon had time to retaliate, Kate got to her feet, all five-foot-practically-nothing, and looked up at Simon, who towered above her. She stood very close to him, confrontationally close, with a hard look on her pretty face.

'I'm a new friend of Amy's, but she's told me quite a lot about you, and I can see that her description was bang on.' She fixed him with a steely gaze that surprised Amy and somehow seemed more impressive coming from such a chubby little face than it would have if she had been tall and lean cheeked. 'I did *not* like what I heard, so why don't you bugger off *right now* and leave her in peace - or I'll tell the management you're harassing her. And don't think I don't mean it. I've dealt with bullies before, and I'm not intimidated by men like you.'

Totally taken aback Simon was silent for a long moment as he stared down at Kate's unflinching eyes, then he grinned. 'Well, well - aren't you a surprising little butterball! But OK, I'll leave you two in peace.'

He turned on his heel and walked away without another glance at Amy. Kate sat down again, met Amy's stunned gaze and said calmly, 'So get your phone out and block him - right away. I know his type, and I bet he'll try to call you later and say how much he enjoyed being bullied by a butterball. You might as well take action right away.'

'God, I'm so sick of this!' Amy frowned and ran a distracted hand through her thick hair. 'He can't stand that I broke it off, not him, but doesn't it seem crazy that he still feels he has to punish me for it?'

'Of course it's not, don't be silly! He lost a trophy, and it doesn't reflect well on his self-image, he's obviously that kind of man. He wants to be envied, looked up to. You were a valued possession that proved something about him.' Kate drank some coffee and put her cup down with a little bang. 'And what's that look for? I'm right, you know. I understand what his kind of man needs to fuel his ego and what upsets them most. And something they see as losing face in public drives them crazy.'

'What's the trophy? You mean, like having a partner? Surely not!'

Kate looked half impatient and half disbelieving, as if she thought Amy had lost her mind and shook her head. 'Don't you get it? *You* are the trophy and he's furious you walked away from him because you've made him doubt his power, and it reflects on his reputation and his self-esteem. He knows you've told people you were the one who broke it off and the slight to his ego makes him to want to punish you.' She paused for a brief moment and added, 'That approach of his had nothing to do with loving you and wanting you back – it was all about him trying to upset you, even scare you – a power play.'

Amy looked carefully at her friend and tried to work out what the joke was, because she could see the corners of Kate's mouth twitching as if she was trying not to laugh. 'You *really* don't get it?' Now Kate was laughing out loud. 'I can't believe it! Don't you have a mirror at home? Every time I've waited for you to arrive, or we've walked somewhere together, I see all these male eyes swivelling to get a proper look at you. Definitely a trophy!'

'But I never think of myself as a trophy,' protested Amy. 'I'm not one of those precious women who take selfies and carry on about their appearance and wear false eyelashes. I'm a serious person – well, mostly.'

Kate shook her head again. 'God, you're not quite of this world, are you? How is life on planet Amy these days? I hope the climate's OK! Now listen - it doesn't matter how you see yourself, it's how others see you. You've got something that attracts attention, particularly from men, and that makes you a trophy whether you like it or not. It's not just the spectacular hair, it's that thing they used to call sex appeal – probably it's got a new trendier name now but never mind.' She reached across and patted Amy's hand. 'And to change the subject, did you read the latest Benson column? He got stuck into the diet industry and though I'm nearly always on a diet myself, I must say it was hilarious.'

'I don't know that column, so no, I didn't read it, but I did read an interesting article about neuroscience on the BBC website – no, I'm not joking this time. It wasn't about little voices in your head, but about how to improve your memory. The key is talking aloud to yourself.'

'Really? How does that work?'

'It's called auditory memory – it's like you recall things better if you've heard them spoken, even if it's your own voice.'

'And *does* it work?'

'I've tried it several times, and it certainly works for me. You know that thing when you go to get something in another room and when you get there you can't remember what it was? Telling yourself aloud *before* you start walking towards it does the trick.'

When they left Amy managed to not turn her head to see where Simon was, or if he was still there. As they parted outside to go their separate ways she reached out and for the first time pulled Kate into a proper hug. 'Thank you! That intervention was as impressive as it was unexpected. I can't thank you enough!'

2

_A_s Amy walked slowly across Hyde Park she continued to think of what Kate had said. Was there really such a thing as sex appeal? Something independent of looks or style, some elusive quality that others could see even if the person, like Amy herself, had no idea they gave off this invisible substance called sex appeal. Could someone like herself, who aside from her attention grabbing hair was just ordinarily pretty and in her own opinion not particularly sexy, have that elusive quality? Then something clicked in her mind, and she came to a halt staring unseeingly at the Peter Pan statue and realised her mistake. If she hadn't been thinking of herself in isolation this would have occurred to her right from the start, but of course the sex appeal thing worked whatever someone looked like. It had nothing to do with looks, either someone had it, or they didn't, even if they weren't aware of it themselves. She could probably list half a dozen men she had known or seen in films, who weren't handsome of even particularly nice looking, but who were very sexy. I must remember to tell Kate next time I see her – how could I doubt her when she is so often right and so totally sensible? It was just that I'd never thought of myself like that, and if she hadn't mentioned it would never have occurred to me. Satisfied now, Amy gave Peter Pan a little salute and continued on her way.

Standing on the platform at the South Kensington underground station Amy replayed the incident in the cafe in her mind and marvelled again at Kate, who had so surprisingly turned out to be able to handle domineering Simon. It wasn't until she was on the train that she began to feel uneasy about the coincidence of Simon being in the cafe at the Victoria and Albert Museum, where she and Kate had started meeting for coffee or lunch once a fortnight. She had never been there before she met Kate, and it was hard to believe Simon had either, not his type of place at all. As the train rocketed through the tunnels her suspicions gradually became impossible to ignore, so she got her phone out and started searching her settings, because if there was a tracking app on her phone no icon showed on her screen. By the time she had changed trains twice and arrived at her destination, she had found and deleted a tracking app called Find Me. Looking up every few seconds to avoid walking into lamp posts, she did some online research on her way to her father's shop and learnt that with that app on her phone her whereabouts could be checked from a nominated person's phone or computer at any time. Simon must have put it on her phone while they were still together, and ever since he'd been able to check where she went.

'That bastard!' she exclaimed and met the amused eyes of a man coming towards her. She slid the phone back into her shoulder bag and blessed Kate yet again.

Several hours later, back in her apartment in Islington, after helping her father sort out his antique shop's accounts, she shrugged off her jacket with a relieved sigh and went to put a frozen dinner in the microwave oven for a late meal. What a strange day! The way Kate had vanquished Simon was possibly the most surprising thing she had ever seen, and she must text her and tell her that there had been a tracking app on her phone, and how she would never have thought of it if Kate hadn't talked about her friend with the devious husband. With a glass of wine in her hand Amy stood by the balcony door and looked across at the two longboats that had tied up at the side of the canal just outside her block of flats a couple of days ago. There were lights in the windows and for the first time she wondered what it would be like to live on a longboat. More or less self-contained, fees to be paid at locks and various service places but no rates and the freedom to move location. In her mind she continued exploring the concept of living on a boat and thought she must check in the morning if they had solar panels on the cabin roof. The whole idea suddenly seemed enticing, even exciting.

She sipped her wine and gradually felt calmer after the welter of emotions of this strange day, the tension and embarrassment of the scene in the café that morning and then the fury of finding that app on her phone. The feeling of outrage had crouched in the back of her mind right through the time she spent with her father. The knowledge that for at least two years her privacy had been invaded, and she had been under surveillance by Simon made her not only angry but also feeling vulnerable, but even as she acknowledged to herself how angry she was, she couldn't help smiling. The memory of Kate getting to her feet, dominating Simon and sending him on his way in no uncertain terms, like a chubby but severe little judge, was the perfect antidote to brooding.

She sat down to eat dinner with a new book loaded on her Kindle, but her mind was drifting and concentration evaded her, so she put the Kindle down and opened her laptop to read what she had written that morning. Good enough, she thought, and paused to consider how to move the story the next step forward. Thinking about Kate had given her an idea, and she jotted down a few words to remind herself. Sometimes ideas came to her as if she had written a whole chapter in her head without being aware of it, and sometimes a fragment of an idea turned up out of the blue, but if she didn't write it down she knew it would have dissolved into thin air a day or two later when she tried to remember it.

Her kind of romantic novels weren't to everybody's taste, which she had always known and the reason she had chosen to publish them under an assumed name. She had fun writing them and that was all that mattered. And maybe the fact that she had never been in a truly trusting and satisfying relationship had something to do with it, she thought, surprised now that this had never occurred to her before. Running past boyfriends through her mind she labelled them each in turn: sexy but boring, kind and unreliable, gorgeous and unfaithful and then Simon, gorgeous, generous, controlling and passive-aggressive. Four serious boyfriends didn't seem a lot at her age considering the first one was when she was fifteen or sixteen, and not one live-together relationship.

As if conjured up by Amy's thoughts about her, Kate called just as Amy was getting ready to go to bed. 'Sorry to call so late,' she said briskly. 'I'm in bed and I simply can't rest until I've talked to you about what you said today. It's been on an endless loop in my head all day and it's driving me crazy. What *did* you mean by when you said, "I can smell him"? Does he smell of something very subtle that you picked up even from that distance – and in the middle of coffee and food smells? I didn't smell anything special.'

'Of course not,' said Amy and went to sit in her favourite armchair and put her feet on the footstool. 'It's not as if *you* have a connection to him, is it? But with my history of him, naturally I smelt him. Hot oil – like something really overheated in a wok.'

There was a disconcerting silence from Kate and Amy chuckled. 'Don't tell me you expect to smell other people's attractions or connections or whatever it is that causes it. I only smell my own.'

'You're kidding, right? This is some elaborate joke of yours again, isn't it? And you expect me to fall for it.'

More confused every moment Amy wondered if Kate had perhaps had a glass too many. 'Kate,' she said apologetically. 'Please don't take this wrong, but have you had a bit much to drink? I just can't work out what it is you're asking – or why?'

'God, no! I haven't had a single glass of wine today – but let's go back to the start. You sat there with your back to the entrance, and suddenly you looked upset and said "I can smell him, he's somewhere near" or something like it. And then you turned your head towards the entrance and there he was. And now you tell me he smells of hot cooking oil! Could you please explain, because I don't understand any of this and as I said, if you don't explain I'll get no sleep tonight – it really is driving me crazy.'

'Listen,' said Amy slowly, trying to work out what was really going on. 'You know how some men give off a scent of something if they're someone you fancy, or even if you are going to fancy them later, but you don't know it yet? And also some men you're really close to, top level friends. Always the same scent for the same person, like a signature. And Simon always gave off that weird hot oil smell from the very first time I met him.' She laughed quietly and added before Kate could say anything, 'It should have made me cautious, shouldn't it? Right from the start I found it odd, it was such an unpleasant smell - but he was really lovely that first time, and he didn't reveal his nasty side for ages.'

'I never got a smell like that from anyone in my life! So it's like a signature, a particular smell for one person? It sounds mad.' Amy could tell how doubtful Kate found her explanation, and though she didn't understand why, it made her feel she must add some extra detail.

'My friend Pete – who's gay and I don't fancy him, but we're very close friends – he smells like lemon grass. I reckon I could track him down in a crowd by that delicious smell. 'His was the first one I identified, so to speak – after I had a bad concussion, that's when this started. And I always presumed a lot of other people had this too, that mine was a bit late in arriving and possibly linked to the concussion.'

Another long silence from Kate, but Amy could

think of nothing else to say. Maybe Kate simply didn't have the ability herself, and she had never realised it existed? Or perhaps she's never fancied anyone, though it seemed unlikely that she had reached her late thirties without any love episodes at all. 'Don't worry about it,' she said now. 'Maybe you just don't have it – there must be people who are born without it and never develop it, whatever it's called. The scent signature, perhaps? I don't think I've ever talked about it before, so I'm not sure if it's common or not. Maybe it's like people who can taste even the tiniest trace of a certain spice? An innate kind of talent – a super-sense.'

They ended the call, and Amy dismissed the conversation as odd, but not in a worrying way, just a bit surprising, until four days later Kate called again.

'Sorry to bang on about this smell signature thing again, but you've got me really interested now,' she said briskly. 'I've been doing some quite extensive research since our conversation the other night and I think maybe you're unique. Nobody's ever heard to the smell thing before.'

'How many people have you asked? Two – or three? Maybe everyone doesn't have it – as I said, I've never thought of it before.' Amy tried to sound reasonable, but really, wasn't this a bit over the top? And very unlike Kate to be so persistent about something so unimportant.

'I've done a mass survey after first asking half a dozen people at work. I didn't mention you, I just casually asked how many had heard of this and the answer was *nobody*! So then I searched the internet, and then I sent out a questionnaire to roughly twenty friends by email and the result was the same – nobody's ever heard about it. Not one single person! How many people do *you* know who have this ability?'

"Oh, for God's sake! How would I know? I don't think I've ever discussed it in my life until you asked me about it. It's just one of those things I've taken for granted – I don't go around talking about it.'

Kate chuckled. 'You've got some weird thing that nobody else has, something so strange it's nearly unbelievable, and you think it's nothing special! But I'm fascinated and I want to know more. And by the way, if I hadn't heard you make that comment about hot oil before you even spotted Simon I'd never believe this talent of yours. Amazing!' Before Amy could reply she added, 'And now I want to know more! Why can you smell Pete's signature if you've never been attracted to him – and you say have known him for years, so it's not as if you're going to fall in love with him now, is it?'

'It's not just about men I might fall in love with,' said Amy and tried to sound casual as if this wasn't a slightly worrying conversation. 'It's just some men. It seems to be those I could or have formed a close bond with.' She paused and tried to work it out in her mind. 'Maybe it's a kinship thing, like knowing before I've even talked to them. Oh no, then I wouldn't have smelt the hot oil from Simon, or maybe I would?' She sighed. 'Hell, Kate - I don't know! But it's always men, and each time it doesn't last, it's like once I've noticed them or looked at them it stops until the next time. I've just realised while we've been talking.'

'It's a paranormal thing!' Kate was laughing now. 'That silly kind of thing I have spent my entire life ridiculing as nonsense - and here it is right in front of me. My God, you're such a special person, and how lucky I am to know you!'

That night Amy couldn't go to sleep, so she finally got up and made a cup of tea, hoping a distraction like re-reading what she had written would make her tired enough to go to sleep. But she ended up sitting in front of her laptop staring at the screen without focus, deep in an internal discussion about the phenomenon she now thought of the "smell signature".

What if nobody else had it? What did it mean? The idea that she was paranormal she dismissed as nonsense, but she couldn't think of anything else that explained it. And it's weird, she mused, that I can smell a signature from random strangers, and sometimes I don't know who it's coming from, but I know it's not just a smell, it comes from a man. I never thought about that when I was talking to

Kate, so I didn't tell her. It made her laugh to think of what Kate's expression would be if she told her about the incident on the tube train a couple of months ago. How she had stood there ready to get out as soon as the doors opened at the next stop and got a strong whiff of caramelised onion and how she knew without thinking that it wasn't someone carrying a packet of take-out food, it came from a person, a man. Not that she knew which man, but there was someone in that carriage who could potentially become close to her or maybe fancied her, it was perfectly clear. She looked around, saw nobody she recognised and decided it was a stranger she would never meet again, and until now she had forgotten about it.

3

*P*arty invitations from Amy's cousin Melissa were rare and often involved large gatherings, sometimes with so many guests you could hardly move through the rooms. Melissa and Aidan entertained at long and seemingly random intervals and preferred repaying past hospitality from a lot of people in one go. It seemed counter-intuitive to Amy because catering and moving furniture for a dinner for forty people was so much more work than having a few casual dinners for a smaller number, but when she voiced this comparison Melissa refused to entertain the idea.

'I know that's how it seems to you – but no thanks,' she said. 'You mean one little dinner party every few weeks instead of a huge dinner party once a year or so? But I can't be bothered with all the faffing around, so I wait until we have a goodish number we owe something and then all the fuss seems worthwhile.'

They were talking on the phone, and Amy could picture her frowning at the mere thought of having those more frequent, small dinner parties. 'All that cleaning and tidying and trying to decide what to cook, over and over again – not to mention having to actually *cook*. Food makes me feel completely neurotic, you know that, and I have panic sessions of self-doubt. So, now we're up for more than six months of reciprocation and I'm already lying awake at night worrying about it.'

'Oh, for heaven's sake, Melissa!' Amy stifled the urge to laugh and ran her free hand up through the back of her hair and held it up to allow cool air to circulate around her neck. 'What's so difficult about it? I just don't get it but never mind. Why don't we plan the food together? And then I'll come over on the day or maybe evening day before, and we'll do the preparations in no time. I know Aidan won't be any help, he'll either be playing golf or have his head buried in some spreadsheet or something. These finance guys are all the same.'

'Would you really do that again? Oh God, that would be wonderful, and you're so efficient. We've got a whole week, so we can sort it out over the phone for a start, and then I'll go shopping if you help me make the list. Remember how last time we did the actual cooking on the day, and it worked out great. Thank you, darling! You're an absolute star.'

So now, on a promising looking Saturday a week later, with early summer sunshine and warmth, Amy dropped the little bag with her good clothes on the floor in Melissa's front hall and gave her a hug. 'Right, where do we start? Is the place tidy, bathroom sparkling? OK, great! Do you want to set out everything on the table before we start cooking like we did last time? Has Aidan got all the wine and the mixers?'

Melissa nodded once for each rapid-fire question. 'Yes all those things are done. I've even bought two packets of paper serviettes and put all the reserve wine glasses through the dishwasher. Let's start with the table – I always feel calmer when that's done, like I'm in control of the day.'

Once again Amy and Melissa worked well together as they had a few times in the past. By five that afternoon everything was under way and only needed the final touches, the table was extended to its full length, and everything was set out on it, the drinks trolley was loaded and carefully positioned in the shade on the terrace. Aidan came home from golf, offered to do whatever was needed, and having been told they didn't need him he went off to watch sport on Sky.

'I don't really mind,' said Melissa in a pretend aside, intended for Aidan to hear. 'I know he seems useless at times, but he's such a good provider, he earns tonnes more than I do - and he's a demon in bed. What else could a girl wish for?'

They looked at each other and laughed at this constant refrain whenever Aidan's domestic shortcomings came up in their conversations, but

Amy knew that their two boys were at an expensive boarding school and at least some of that comment was true.

By half past six the three of them were sitting on the covered terrace with a glass of chilled champagne congratulating themselves on the perfect evening and how gorgeous the garden was with the early summer flowers in full bloom. 'And let's face it, this season so far has been so random.' Melissa gestured at the colourful display in the garden. 'Such a mix of warm and cold, but perhaps the rain now and then has made this possible. Lucky tonight is so warm – it would have been a real squeeze to fit everyone inside.'

By half past seven the garden was noisy with talk and laughter, the food was heating, and the kitchen bench was full of bowls and dishes covered with tea towels.

Who would have thought thirty-six people could make so much noise? thought Amy and looked out from the terrace. It sounds like a hundred. And look, isn't it funny? That burnt orange must be trendy at the moment – I can see three women and one man wearing it. Very striking, but I couldn't get away with it.

People moved from one group to another, put their glass down and forgot where and came inside for another one. As the time for the buffet dinner approached Amy walked quietly around picking up abandoned glasses and platters and took them to the kitchen, where she filled the dishwasher and started it. Absently she registered a smell of freshly brewed coffee and had only just thought "where did that come from?" when a voice said, 'Can you pause that thing and open it? I've got another four glasses and a bowl I found in the gazebo.'

Aha, she thought, that's where it came from, that's the first coffee scent man I've ever come across.

Behind her stood an unbelievably goodlooking man, and Amy couldn't help smiling at him. The whole package, great body and thick black hair, which combined with the face of a naughty little boy was irresistible. Sparkling blue eyes met hers and she noted the designer stubble at the prescribed length – not so long as to resemble a close-cropped beard and not so short as to make him look unshaven. Not someone she had met before, but the kind of eye candy that never goes amiss at a party.

He put the four wine glasses in the dishwasher and waited while she closed and restarted it. 'I'm Patrick.' He held out his hand. 'I don't think we've met before. I'm a friend of Aidan's from golf. I noticed you outside - I couldn't take my eyes off your fabulous hair. What's your connection?'

'Melissa's my cousin, but tonight I'm also her kitchen helper. Let's go outside away from this noisy thing.'

From then on Patrick seemed to be close by wherever she went, and when the time came for everyone to help themselves from the buffet table in the dining room he was right beside her, so they ended up sitting together at one of the tables in the garden. At the end of the evening Patrick appeared beside her, once again accompanied by the smell of coffee. She was standing under the tree with strings of tiny lights strung along the branches talking to a woman she had met once before, and they were both looking up. 'I love this tree – it's got the perfect structure to have those lights.'

'I agree,' said Patrick and tilted his head back. 'Like a light sculpture and much nicer than those hanging lanterns everyone had a few years ago.'

The woman Amy had been talking to laughed. 'Everyone loves this tree, apart from my husband who says he can't abide garden decorations.'

They agreed this was a pity and the woman left to get herself another glass of wine, and Patrick asked if he could put his number in Amy's phone. 'Then you can text me and I'll have your number - and maybe we can meet for a drink sometime.'

'Of course,' said Amy and handed over her phone which was in the pocket of her white wide-legged trousers. So practical to have pockets, she thought, while Patrick put his number in, and this is perfect because I need never text him if I decide I don't want to see him again.

At quarter to two in the morning, Melissa, Aidan and Amy sat in the living room with bowls of left-over Channel Island strawberries and cream, exhausted and having had slightly too much wine.

'Wasn't it lucky we had a really warm evening finally? Hardly anyone retreated inside when it got dark. It all went so well,' said Melissa and pointed her spoon at Amy. 'Thanks to you! Without you it would have been awful, and I would have been super stressed and not enjoyed anything. We'll clean up the mess in the morning, and you'd better call a cab before you fall asleep – your eyelids are drooping. I'm surprised you didn't leave with Mr Super Sexy. I noticed him hovering around you all night.'

'He seems quite nice.' Amy yawned. 'Apart from that mirror thing.'

'What mirror thing?' asked Aidan, who from looking half asleep suddenly seemed interested in the conversation, and Amy made a face and shook her head in disbelief. 'It was amazing – first I caught him checking his appearance in the big mirror over the fireplace - making a tiny adjustment to his fabulous hair. And when he took my phone to put his number in, he checked his appearance in the reflection of the screen after he turned it off to hand it back to me. A very vain man, so pleased with his good looks.'

'You know what he does, don't you?' Now the corners of Aidan's mouth were twitching. 'He's a *very* highly paid model, top level. Often seen on TV commercials behind the wheel of a mega expensive car or escorting a beautiful woman into a casino or a fancy restaurant. He lives on his looks so to speak. But he plays a very good game of golf.'

'Ah well, that makes everything OK then, and I'll forgive the vanity.' Amy yawned and got to her feet. 'But I must get my little bag from the spare room now - the Uber will be here any second.'

'I don't know why you never stay the night.' Melissa yawned in sympathy. 'You could go straight to bed here and then home in the morning.'

Amy made no reply, just hugged them both and left. She had no intention of confessing how much she hated the thought of waking up in someone else's house and having to share their morning routine, even a cousin she had been close to all her life. Which was why she had never agreed to live with Simon, who had wanted her to come and live at his place in Lancaster Gate, a much bigger apartment than hers. Not to mention what a prestigious address he had compared to hers. His was the kind of flat that must always be referred to as an apartment, one she would never be able to afford herself, but it still hadn't tempted her. She couldn't face the prospect of losing the privacy to write, to not be able to just sit down at her laptop when a whole chapter unexpectedly appeared in her head and needed to be typed into the current book as fast as possible. Quite apart from the strange feeling she had right from the start of her relationship with Simon, that living together would be a commitment she was not prepared to make.

4

After thinking about it for nearly two weeks Amy texted Patrick and asked if he was up for a drink after work on the Friday that week. His reply came back nearly instantly and made her wonder if there was something wrong with him, if maybe women didn't want to date him for some reason. But Melissa and Aidan hadn't indicated that they knew anything about him other than positive qualities, he was gainfully employed, played a good game of golf and was extremely handsome. They hadn't even reacted in a negative way when she mentioned how many times she had noticed Patrick checking himself in a mirror or some other reflective surface, as if being a model explained it to their satisfaction. Let's face it, thought Amy, it's still vanity on a huge scale, but never mind, he might be fun.

They met at Amy's favourite bistro three blocks from her flat, and though she kept her eyes on him she didn't catch him studying his own image once, so maybe what she had noticed at Melissa's party was a temporary aberration. It was hard to imagine someone who looked like Patrick feeling insecure about his appearance, but it was difficult to think what else it could have been.

Disappointingly, he turned out to be less interesting than she had hoped, and they seemed to have few things in common. When she got home after two glasses of wine and a meal of tapas, she made a little mental list of his good points. He was cheerful and had a huge supply of amusing stories about his various modelling jobs and the famous people he had met at events, but that was as far as it went. She had tried to introduce the topic of books by asking what he was reading at the moment, but it turned out that Patrick rarely read books, he usually only read magazines, watched detective series on TV or YouTube videos about cars. He liked cooking, which Amy didn't, though she was efficient in a kitchen when she had to be. He knew a lot about films and wasn't interested in current affairs, but he had an ironic sense of humour, which was always a good thing in a man, and his humour was often at his own expense. She knew that going out with him would not lead to anything apart from light entertainment. His astounding good looks was an advantage if all you wanted to do was gaze at him, but after a few dates she would probably be so used to his handsome face that it would cease to register. But for the time being she was happy to see him again, and it made a nice change from a demanding job.

She told Kate about Patrick over Saturday lunch, and Kate asked why on earth she would consider going out with him again if they had nothing in common and if there was no prospect of a long term relationship.

'For heaven's sake, Kate, of course it's worth it.' Amy tamped down a smile that tried to emerge. 'Just *imagine* what it will do for my reputation. I'll take selfies with him and post them on social media and people will admire me for having attracted such a gorgeous and well-known man! It will raise my standing for sure. I might even sign up to TikTok and post little video clips of us having cocktails or hugging.'

For a moment Kate was taken in by this shallow explanation, then she burst out laughing. 'Oh no, no - you're not going to catch me out like that again. I'm getting to know these evil tactics of yours. You're just doing a selfie-queen impersonation, aren't you? Have you got a photo of him I can have a look at?'

'No, but I can show you what he looks like if you really want to see.' Amy got her phone out and searched for the car video Patrick had mentioned over their drinks, a TV advertisement he had made a few months ago which he was very proud of. As he had said, it had been very exciting to see the finished product because in the shots from outside the car it looked as if he was driving extremely fast on a winding road through a forest and sliding around corners, when it was really a stunt driver doing the driving. At the time Amy had failed to see why this would make him feel pleased with himself, but it was probably due to how concerned he was with his looks and reputation. She found the video clip and passed the phone to Kate.

'Oh, him!' exclaimed Kate. 'He seems to be everywhere when someone's trying to promote cars that cost millions or underpants that cost as much as a fridge. He's obviously the perfect tool for parting wealthy people from their money, those who want to be up there with the best and the most.'

They both laughed, but after a moment Amy felt mean and said seriously, 'But he's kind and attentive, and he has quite a wicked sense of humour, so he's good company. We shouldn't laugh at him.'

After a few casual dates for drinks and dinners Amy felt she had Patrick's measure. She would never be more than friends, but she found herself looking forward to seeing him again each time they made a date. Though they didn't have shared interests he was entertaining and very kind, and probably exactly what she needed as light relief after a few tough weeks of overwork and stress. The fact that they had hired another accountant to train had not yet made an impression on her workload.

. . .

The restaurant Patrick had suggested this time was yet another one where Amy had never been before, but she had seen it mentioned many times online and in magazines, and it was probably hideously expensive. A place where famous, or hoping to be famous, people would line up to get in, but apparently Patrick could book a table at short notice, which was probably a measure of how desirable he was as a customer. They met outside and as they walked into the restaurant he took her hand, which surprised her, the first physically affectionate gesture he had made and not something she had expected. As they were shown to their table people waved to him or called out, so obviously he was a regular customer and knew all the so-called right people.

When they got up to leave after a delectable dinner, which Patrick insisted on paying for, saying the place was his choice and therefore he would foot the bill, she was beginning to feel certain the vague suspicion she had had for a couple of weeks was right. On the way out he put his arm casually around her shoulders and pulled her close to his side, and Amy knew this display affection was for show, but she let him lead her out through the door held open for them and said nothing about it until they were safely away from the restaurant.

'Nice place and gorgeous food. Thank you, Patrick - I really enjoyed that. Such a treat!'

'That's good!' said Patrick and let his arm drop from her shoulder. 'I'm glad you liked it. I go there quite often - it's one of the best places to be seen.'

Amy nearly laughed but decided that rather than display amusement she would try to find out for a fact what was behind this strange little interlude of hand holding and shoulder hugging. Would he admit what she suspected?

'What do you mean by the best place to be seen? Do you go there so other people can see you have enough money to eat there or what?'

Patrick replied casually without any particular emphasis or any sign of embarrassment. 'It's important in my job that I'm seen in the right places. It kind of proves that I'm still a desirable property. I know it sounds silly, and I do like the food there too, of course. But the main reason I go, is for people to see me with a lovely woman - and also for it to be understood that I can afford to eat there as often as I want to.'

After a moment's silence while Amy stifled laughter, she said, hoping she sounded serious, 'That's obviously important for your career, I can see that. So, I'm a kind of accessory?'

Standing there on the pavement in the warm summer night, with people walking past on either side of them, Amy studied Patrick's face while he thought for a surprisingly long time, and when he did reply he sounded slightly embarrassed. 'Well, you're not *just* an accessory, you're a close friend now. I mean, I do love meeting up with you and we have fun together. But I must admit that if you weren't so noticeable and so gorgeous I probably wouldn't have asked you out to start with. I hope you don't mind me being honest, but you did ask. And now that I've discovered what fun you are, I'd like to continue going out – if you don't mind, as I said. Romance is out, though.'

They started walking again while Amy decided that her suspicion was confirmed, so she decided to be completely honest and ask the question she would probably not have asked before they started this conversation.

'Are you by any chance a closet gay? Are we going out so you can maintain a straight image in the media and amongst people who matter to your career? And if that's the case, *why* does it matter?'

Patrick stopped, put his hand on her arm and turned her to face him. For the first time since she had met him, he looked very serious, his eyes were fixed on hers as if he was making sure that what he was going to say would be taken at face value, a serious statement.

'No, I'm not gay, but I have practically no libido. I have low testosterone levels and some other issues. I'm simply not interested in sex, and I don't need it, though I can do it – sometimes. Officially I'm classified as *asexual*, though that doesn't mean much. My agent gets me a lot of jobs of the kind where women fancy me, so I'm under strict instructions to be seen with attractive women regularly. I hope you're not feeling insulted.'

That made her laugh outright. 'I'll tell you something funny,' she said. 'A while ago a friend of mine told me that men look at me as if I'm desirable, she said I was like a trophy to them, and of course I didn't believe her. I'd never thought of myself as a trophy, and I didn't know that men look at me in the street, not any more than they look at any other woman. It's flattering that you think I'm desirable enough to enhance your reputation, and I don't mind being an accessory at all.'

'You don't? Not even now when you know it's not going to lead to anything exciting – like sex?'

He sounded as if he couldn't quite believe it, which made her laugh again and put her hand on his arm. 'No, of course I don't mind. I've never been sexually attracted to you, so I'm not insulted, and not particularly surprised either. I wondered once or twice if you were gay - or bisexual perhaps - so nothing much has changed.'

He put his hand on hers and gave it a little squeeze. 'So, will you go out with me now and again - now that you know this? Like a pretend romance?'

'God, yes, of course I will! If you keep taking me to places like that for dinner *and* pay the bill, I'll be very happy to go out with you. The perfect kind of useful friendship. And don't take that the wrong way – I really do enjoy your company, and we have the same sense of humour, which is a great thing to bond over.'

They grinned at each other, and Patrick raised his hand and hailed a cab. 'I'll call you next week.'

In the car on the way home she thought of how she had smelt coffee when he appeared behind her at Melissa's dinner party and how she should have known he was a special person. It always meant something when a man had what she and Kate had decided to call a "smell signature" – she would either find the man in question attractive, maybe go out with him or have a relationship, or they would become close friends. Since her intense conversation about it with Kate she had realised it was only a few men she could smell from a distance, never women. And thinking about it instead of just taking it for granted had also made her realise that a smell signature could have a meaning. Simon and the hot oil smell, for example. That should have warned her about him before she even spoke to him the first time. How could a man whose advance scent was overheated oil be anything but a threat? And lovely Patrick smelling of freshly ground coffee, such a nice comforting thing, so obviously it should have told her straight off that they would be good friends.

Lunch at Pete's place

Amy looked at herself in the mirror unable to take her eyes off herself in the dress she had bought a couple of days ago, a simple dress but a colour she had never worn before. The reason she had bought it at all was due to a comment Kate had made when they had lunch the previous week. They were meeting for coffee or lunch nearly every weekend now instead of every two or three weeks. Somehow their friendship had matured into something deeper after that memorable incident at the museum café, when Simon interrupted their coffee morning. Kate, who never wore anything trendy or smart herself and usually dressed in loose-fitting clothes in dark colours, had surprisingly turned out to have impeccable dress sense and often commented cleverly on what other women wore. Amy had mentioned that she must get something new to wear for social occasions now that she went out for dinner so often, but she hated shopping and having to make decisions, so she often gave up and went home without having bought anything. And Kate had made a comment that at the time had seemed to come out of left field, but now Amy realised that Kate had taken note of what she tended to wear and decided to give her some advice.

'With your dark red hair and very pale skin you could try aubergine,' she had said quite casually. 'I don't mean bright purple but the colour of the aubergine fruit, that dark purply-nearly-black colour. I think it would go well with your hair and skin.' Then she had changed the subject, as if what she had said was of no real importance and asked if Amy had watched the new Danish drama series on Netflix everyone was talking about. The comment came back to Amy when she stood in a dress shop two days later, hesitating about where to start, despondently thinking of what a chore this was. But suddenly "aubergine" popped into her mind, and she started looking for the colour. She found the dress in the fourth shop she went to and bought it despite the hideous price, "not far off the national debt" as she described it to Kate in a text message.

Now Amy looked at herself in the mirror and thought that Kate's comment had been very clever, giving her a hint without any pressure. What a wonderful friend she was! Simon had always tried to make her dress what he referred to as smarter, which usually meant that he wanted her to wear things that attracted more attention.

'You're too casual, my treasure,' he would say. 'You could make more of yourself.' Which in retrospect supported Kate's comment that to Simon Amy was a trophy, an object that others might envy, and which boosted his self-esteem. She had never taken much notice of his comments about how she dressed, probably because she didn't particularly want to attract attention, but looking at herself now in the full length mirror she felt as if the dress was changing her personality. It's making me more confident, she thought, it makes me feel as if I wouldn't mind a room full of people turning to look at me, so different from the way I usually feel. All those times with Patrick and people staring in bars and restaurants, that was due to him, and it didn't make me more confident, but now I feel different, very different.

· · ·

After a frustratingly slow trip Amy arrived very late at Pete's flat in Southwark feeling guilty as he had said that this time he was making it a proper sit-down lunch, a bit more formal, because he was introducing his new partner to those who hadn't yet met him.

'I'm sorry I'm so late,' she said and hugged him. 'I hope I haven't held up lunch. Something happened on the line, and we sat in the tunnel for ages waiting for them to get something off the tracks.'

'Probably a body,' said Pete casually. 'And don't worry, we're still waiting for some others.' He pushed her further into the flat, which was one of Amy's favourite places, tiny but perfect. A lovely modern flat built like a little self-contained house on top of a converted warehouse with a spacious roof garden.

'Go out on the terrace and someone will give you a glass of whatever you want to drink. I've got to go and help Roger in the kitchen - he's a fabulous cook but very messy, so he needs a kitchenhand hovering, ready to tidy up as he goes, or the place becomes chaotic. I wish they'd made the kitchen just a bit bigger – there's not enough bench space for someone like Roger.' He gestured towards the terrace. 'There's no wind today and warm enough to eat outside, so I thought I'd take the opportunity to have a whole crowd while the forecast is good. And you look stunning, by the way. I should have said first up, sorry! Gorgeous dress!'

Amy went through the sliding glass doors to the

roof garden where two long tables had been set for a sit-down lunch under the large shade sails Pete put up every spring. Pausing just outside the door to look around she saw a few people she knew, all busy talking in small groups, so she walked over to the bar table against the outside wall where bottles and glasses were arranged. I need a drink right away after that dreadful journey, she thought, something cold and refreshing. As she stood there studying the bottles a strong smell of cinnamon enveloped her, and she turned.

'Can I pour you a drink?' asked the man who had just come up behind her. 'You look as if you've just arrived.'

'I only just got here, nearly didn't arrive at all.' Amy smiled up at the burly man in front of her. 'The train stopped in a tunnel, and we just sat there for nearly an hour before it got going again.'

'Debris on the line,' said the tall man briefly. 'Someone else texted and said they'd been held up too – they arrived just before you. And by the way, my name's Ben Anderson. What would you like to drink?'

With a glass of white wine in her hand Amy moved slightly to one side, intensely aware of the ripple of something-or-other that had flowed up her arm when his hand touched hers when he handed her the glass. Not something that had happened to her before, and she had always wondered if it was an invented sensation when she read about it, though she had used it in her own books. And what was it - lust or a mild charge of static electricity? She took a sip of wine while she studied him over the rim of her glass, quietly assessing him: not my type, too tall and too big. Not that he's fat, just very solid looking. It's like standing beside a cliff, but he'd probably be useful as shelter in a storm.

Aloud she said, 'I'm Amy. Have you known Pete long?'

'We play squash together – have done for eight or nine years. I usually beat him, but don't tell him I told you. And we share another thing, park runs. God knows how many we've done by now, must be dozens.'

'Are they fun? I've never been to a park run event.'

Ben looked as if he had never considered this aspect before. 'I don't know if I'd call them fun, but it's a nice way to get some exercise in the weekend - not too strenuous, but you can run as fast as you like, of course. And parks are always nice. Pete's not a great runner so I usually adapt my pace to his.'

'Perhaps I should try it one day,' said Amy, but she didn't mean it. It wasn't the sort of thing that appealed to her and running with a crowd seemed even less fun than running on your own, though as he said, parks were always nice. Their conversation came to a halt when two people, who knew Amy, joined them and from then on she got involved with others until it was time to sit down for lunch. From where she sat she could see Ben talking to a tall skinny woman further down on the other side of the table and the thought from earlier on recurred. What was that strange feeling when their hands touched? That fizzing sensation running up her arm had been brief but intense, and she couldn't remember ever feeling anything quite like it before. It probably was static electricity, she decided, it had certainly felt like it, but nobody had ever come with a smell of cinnamon before, one of her favourite spices. She mentally shook the speculation off and turned to the man on her right to listen to what he was saying about Pete's new price comparison app for smartphones and forgot about it for the time being.

At the end of the afternoon when the temperature was dropping and a breeze had come up, and after multiple conversations about how long she had known Pete and where they had met, she was trying to decide if she should go straight home or accept the invitation to go with some others to the pub down the road.

But listening to their plans to go on from a drink in the pub to a place with music, Amy decided she would rather go home and was just thanking Pete and Roger for the lovely lunch when she saw Ben heading their way.

'Oh, Amy,' said Roger. 'Have you met the famous Ben? Let me introduce you.'

'We met earlier, when I first arrived.' Amy smiled at Ben. 'At the time I didn't know he was famous, though. Is he famous for doing park runs?'

'He's a political commentator – he's got a weekly syndicated column, and he gets interviewed on radio a lot. And recently he's launched a new column which is already very popular too. I'm so proud of him.'

'I'm sorry to say I don't read political columns very often – I'm very slack when it comes to politics, I'm afraid. Have you two known each other long?'

'He's my cousin, my first cousin,' said Roger beaming with pride. 'Our mothers are sisters and we're all very proud of him – the first famous person in the family.'

5

Just home from work, Amy stood at her kitchen window talking to her friend Charlotte about her ex-husband's new partner when her phone started vibrating in a worrying way. 'Sorry to interrupt, but something weird is happening with my phone – it's vibrating, and I don't know what it means.'

'Have you got it set to vibrate when you get messages? Did anything pop up on your screen?' Charlotte sounded mildly amused. 'If it's set to vibrate when you're on calls or have your phone on mute it probably just means you got a text message while we were talking.'

'Oh, of course! I do have the vibration function on, so I know what going on when I'm in meetings and things and my phone's muted. Just in case it's something I need to respond to sooner rather than later. How funny – I can't ever have had a message come in while I was talking to someone.'

They were discussing the best way of dealing with the upcoming sixth birthday of Charlotte and Roland's daughter, Caroline, and how reluctant Charlotte was to have Roland's new partner at the birthday party. Amy could sympathise to a certain extent, but whatever she had suggested so far had met with little enthusiasm from Charlotte.

'But listen,' she said now, having had a sudden inspiration. 'Don't you think the party is the perfect place for meeting her for the first time in person? Surrounded by kids and parents and lots of noise and distractions – you wouldn't be expected to talk to her for long, would you? You'd be sure to be interrupted. And then that first meeting is over, and you can relax a bit next time.'

'You might be right.' Charlotte sounded half convinced. 'And if no distraction crops up I'll pretend I can see something I need to attend to and dash off. OK, you're right, it would probably work, so long as I don't lose my cool.'

'And don't forget that she's probably just as nervous as you are and expects you to be sarcastic or hostile. You're the wronged woman, after all, and she probably feels guilty.'

'Ha!' said Charlotte grimly. 'And so she damn well should! You know how I told you about how I discovered about their affair – I saw her message on his phone lock screen, and I knew how to get into it.' Amy knows precisely how Chalotte found out, having been told several times before, but the need to repeat it seemed nearly ritualistic, so she listened patiently. 'Loads of messages – five months of passionate sex and I had no idea! I mean, he's had affairs before, but they've always been super short. So, I might feel like being sarcastic when I meet her – at least if she tries to be nice. But she's going to be part of my life now, possibly forever, so I'd better get over it. I'll let you know how it pans out.'

Amy put the phone on the windowsill and contemplated the view over the canal, deep in thought about how different her life was compared to that of some of her married friends. The lack of complications now that Simon couldn't follow her, the freedom to do whatever she wanted to in the weekends and the peaceful calm of her little apartment when she came home from a demanding day at work. Charlotte and Roland's marriage had been fraught with trouble nearly from the start and she wondered how many hours she had spent listening to Charlotte agonising about his intermittent unfaithfulness, his refusal to take his share of parental leave and the way he spent a couple of evenings a week at the squash club.

Amy shook her head at her reflection in the window and went to check what she could have for dinner and forgot all about the text message that had made her phone vibrate while she was talking to Charlotte. It wasn't until she was going to bed after three enjoyable hours buried in her writing that she remembered and went to get the phone from the kitchen windowsill and found a text message from Ben: *Hi Amy, it's Ben Anderson. I got your number from Pete and Roger – hope you don't mind. I tried calling but your phone was busy, and you didn't respond to my voice message. Call me if you feel like meeting for a drink on Friday.*

Once again standing by the window with the phone held limply in her hand she relived that strange moment at Pete's lunch party when Ben's fingers touched hers as he handed her a glass of wine. How she felt a current run up her arm, sudden and unexpected, and how he had been preceded by a waft of cinnamon. Now, she considered him again, this time from a more rational perspective, leaving out the touch and the cinnamon smell. A tall, sturdy man, not particularly handsome, though not ugly either, for whom she had felt no particular attraction at the time. A man who had not displayed any interest in her during their short conversation, but who came with a scent she associated with comfort and enjoyment.

It's just silly, she thought and went to clean her teeth. It's the perfect example of an oxymoron, two parts that contradict each other but still produced a result. But despite how little sense it made, she replied to Ben's text: *I'd love to. Text me when and where and I'll be there.*

When Amy arrived at the Islington bistro he had suggested, Ben was already there. She wondered if he had asked questions about her and found out she lived not far from there, which felt slightly creepy, but she was wrong as she found out as soon as they were seated.

'I was going to suggest that you made the choice, but I was with Pete and Roger the other night and I mentioned I was going to ask you out.' His smile was genuine, he was finding this amusing. 'And Pete told me we live not far from each other – such a coincidence. Did you think I'd been spying on you?'

Amy felt her face colour because that was exactly what she had thought when he suggested Bravo, one of her favourite places to have dinner locally. 'I did wonder – it seemed too good to be true. To be able to walk from my apartment in ten minutes!'

'Took me fifteen,' said Ben. 'But never mind, so long as you know I wasn't being devious. What is that you do?'

With this sudden change of topic, Ben studied her as if he was memorising every feature of her face, an intense scrutiny, but as opposed to when other men did it he didn't make her feel self-conscious. 'I couldn't stop looking at your hair when we met at Pete's, and I completely forgot to ask all those normal questions– like what your job is.'

'I usually ask people to guess.' Amy held back a smile. 'It's always fun to hear what people think I do – it's quite an unusual job and nobody's got it right yet. Well, it isn't really that unusual, but to most people it *seems* unusual.'

'You're a hair model.' Ben's eyes twinkled. 'It's got to have something to do with the way you look, and please don't tell me you're a porn star. Not that I have anything against porn stars, but I think I'd rather you weren't one of them.'

'More unusual than that.' Amy smiled openly in anticipation of his reaction. 'I'm sure there are far more porn stars than forensic accountants in this world, probably on a ratio of a thousand to one.'

'Forensic accountant? Never heard of it. Is there really such a thing or are you joking?'

How many times had she heard people say similar things? It was one of the most common reactions when she told people what her job was. 'Oh yes, it's a real job and a very interesting one if you have an analytical mind and a highly developed sense for detail – and focus, as in the ability to concentrate. It's like being a financial detective.'

He considered this in silence, drank some of his wine and said apologetically, 'I hope you didn't mind that I thought you might be a hair model seeing you're a highly qualified professional. But you've got the most wonderful hair. I don't think I've ever seen such luscious red curls, definitely natural – and such a strong, dark red, not orangey red like a lot of redheads. If you get sick of being a forensic accountant you could moonlight as a model for shampoo.'

'It has been suggested before, but no, it's not

what I want to do. And now you've made me wish I'd remembered to bring my discipline fork, because this is *not* what I want to talk about – such a boring topic.' Amy made a face. 'Oh, wait a minute, it might be in the bottom of my bag. Maybe I didn't take it out after I went to see my rude neighbour the other day.'

'You have a discipline fork? Is it one of those that gives people an electric shock like the cops have? I thought they were illegal. Please don't use it on me.' She could tell he was enjoying this insane conversation; the left corner of his mouth had tweaked up just a tiny bit.

'No, no,' she replied seriously and tried not to laugh. 'It's an ordinary dinner fork, one with particularly sharp points. Perfect for stabbing someone as retribution for being annoying.'

While she was getting ready for bed Amy mentally relived their conversation and in particular the three moments that stood out as significant. The first occurred when they were discussing the Regent's Canal.

'You lucky thing,' Ben said when he realised her flat looked out over the canal. 'I love the canal – it's like a little universe all its own. Longboats that people live on, the towpath where the horses used to trot along pulling the barges before anything had engines. My flat looks out over the back of a big office building that faces a parallel street. Totally uninteresting.'

'It really is lovely, and interesting too – always something to look at and it changes from day to day.' Amy took another sip of the burgundy Ben had recommended. 'God, this wine is nice! But back to the canal – it gives me endless pleasure. I often stand at the windows facing that way and just watch whatever is going on. The other day two girls in kayaks came past and I wondered what would happen if they went through that tunnel and met a boat.'

'Ah, the famous Islington tunnel – do you realise how long it is? Nearly a kilometre – and it's very dark inside. If you look in you can see the little round opening at the other end, but when you're inside it's totally dark.'

'I didn't realise you were allowed to walk through it – I usually go for a walk in the other direction. Or have you been through it on a boat?'

'Swimming,' said Ben and grinned at her expression. 'Probably not approved of, but I had my little safety plan in case a boat came at me from either direction. I was wearing the headlamp I put on when I run in the dark, and I had the so called intermittent setting on, so the red lights both back and front were blinking.' He took in her dubious expression and continued, as if to reassure her. 'I reckoned boats from either direction would notice me close by the wall and be careful. They have to watch carefully to steer straight in the tunnel, after all.'

The second memorable moment was his face when she told him about her job, and finally the best moment of all, though slightly confusing even so: when they parted outside to walk in opposite directions, and he reached out and took hold of her shoulders and leaned in to plant a kiss on her forehead. A very unexpected move and somehow quaint, nearly old-fashioned, but accompanied by the same intense feeling as when their hands touched at Pete's place. Perhaps they would become very good friends as the fizzing touch and the cinnamon smell indicated, not to mention the affectionate forehead kiss, though for some reason the idea of friendship didn't feel right. She told herself to stop over-thinking everything and went to bed.

6

On a perfect late June morning, with a strong, warm breeze and people smiling at each as they met on the sidewalk, Amy walked briskly toward the office enjoying the swish of her new skirt and the way the wind made her hair flow back from her shoulders. Sometimes in the summer months she wondered if she should just cut her hair short and avoid the heavy weight of it making her shoulders and the back of her neck so hot, but today the feeling of her mane of red hair streaming behind her felt wonderful, nearly like flying.

A few hours later with the feeling of the wind in her hair forgotten, Amy studied the grumpy face of Stefan, who owned the firm, whose scowl only very rarely appeared. Grant O'Leary, their new employee, had only started a couple of months ago, but already Stefan was beginning to worry about him.

'Would you please remind me why I hired him – I think we made a mistake.' Stefan tilted his chair back at a dangerous angle, his ruddy face creased in a worried frown. 'I know you didn't like him because he seemed a bit hesitant in the interview, but there wasn't anything really wrong with him, was there?'

'For heaven's sake, why don't you just give the guy a bit of time to settle in?' Amy took a bite of her cream cheese muffin and studied Stefan's face. Was he really worried or just annoyed that Grant had made a couple of silly remarks in the Monday morning work-in-progress meeting? 'And I *didn't* dislike him, not at all. It was just that he seemed unsure of what he wanted in life. But that was your fault for asking that dumb thing about where he wanted to be in five years. I mean, when you interviewed me, I think I said I'd like to be on an island in the Caribbean - and you still hired *me*. Grant just isn't up to speed yet, but he's done a couple of quite complex analysis jobs for me and done them well. His skill with spreadsheets is impressive – he could probably make Excel make a cup of coffee. I'm sure he'll be worth his salary in another month of two.'

'Of course, I hired *you* – clearly super competent and mentally organised, even if you were a bit cheeky. And look at you now, senior analyst and any minute now you'll ask for another pay rise.' He eyed the platter on the boardroom table where what was left over from the meeting's morning tea was now his and Amy's lunch. 'I'm glad they gave us some real food this time instead of all those cakes and stuff they usually send up.' He picked up a club sandwich and looked suspiciously at it.

'You can stop frowning, Stefan! It does *not* have cucumber in it. I called them after George had placed the order and told them to give us real food, no cakes and *no* cucumber.' Amy laughed at his disgruntled face. 'But about Grant - let's just hang in there and see how he develops. I think he's got what it takes to be useful in the not too distant future.'

Suddenly Stefan grinned and his whole face changed. Amazing, thought Amy, when he's grumpy he has the world's grumpiest face and when he laughs he's like Santa mixed with a teddy bear. 'Maybe he used someone else's CV for the interview,' he said now. 'Maybe we've been scammed.'

Amy got up and patted his shoulder as she passed him. 'I've got to go. I'm meeting with a woman from the Fraud Squad in ten minutes so I must find George and get him to clear this table before she arrives.'

Just after dinner that evening Amy's phone pinged with an email alert, but she was busy wiping down the kitchen benches and forgot to check what the message was until she was going to bed, something that often happened if she was busy writing, or if she sat down to watch a TV drama. She sat on the edge of the bed to mute the sound on her phone for the night and saw there was an email from her aunt Susie in New Zealand. Trying to recall when she last corresponded with Susie made her feel ashamed about how long ago it must be, probably over a year. How odd, she thought guiltily, we exchanged a few emails after I got back from my New Zealand holiday two years ago, but somehow it didn't continue – probably my fault.

Dear Amy, I have just found a letter from long ago, which your mother wrote when you were a little girl and which I was supposed to send or give to you on your 30th birthday. The letter was forgotten until I found it today when I was tidying up my house preparatory to moving to an apartment, and now I am worried that if I send it and it gets lost you will never know what your mother wrote to you. We have two options. I can hold on to the letter until you next come to New Zealand, which both I and the boys hope you will do, or I can open the letter and take a photo of the text and e-mail it to you. The date on the envelope is two days before your third birthday, and I can only imagine that it contains something she really wanted you to know. Even six months before she died she might have wanted to make sure that whatever was on her mind didn't get forgotten. I truly have no idea what it might be. We were close as sisters, but some things were probably hard to discuss long distance. She never mentioned what it contained when she mailed it to me and asked me to keep it. Much love, Susie.

How surprising, thought Amy. What could mum possibly have wanted to tell me, but not until I turned thirty? Very mysterious, but I really want to know now. She thought for a moment or two and decided that whatever her mother had written all those years ago might be something that she didn't want to share with others, not with anyone else apart from her daughter, but obviously it was something which that daughter needed to be a mature adult to deal with. After a few minutes' thought Amy responded to Susie's message.

Hi Susie, what an exciting find - I can't wait to read it! Please pop it in a courier envelope and send it. I don't think the risk of it getting lost on the way is very great and I would like to open that envelope myself. Not that I don't trust your discretion, but it would be such a special moment to open an envelope my mother addressed to me and sealed all those years ago. Big hug and love to you and the boys, Amy.

A couple of hours later Amy found it hard to go to sleep after this intriguing little promise of mystery and excitement. Her usual routine of reading herself to sleep didn't work, so after an hour she got up and logged on to the work server and worked on her current project until finally, at quarter to one in the morning she was tired enough to go back to bed.

The morning after Amy received Susie's email she woke to a rainy day with blustery winds and a feeling of apprehension, as if she had forgotten about something threatening. She knew this feeling was rooted in nothing more than vague worry about her mother's letter, but however rational she tried to be, the feeling persisted. Why had her mother written a letter to be given to her on her thirtieth birthday, what could it possibly be that she needed to be properly adult to process?

It was only later, after arriving drenched at the office and with her umbrella discarded in a sidewalk rubbish bin after blowing inside-out, that another and more cheerful thought popped into Amy's head. Perhaps it was advice about children, or stories about Amy's own early childhood, something to tell her own children, not that she had any, but her mother might have thought she would have by the time she was thirty. On and off during the day this theory returned, and by late afternoon it had come to seem not only reasonable but probable.

Amy was talking to George in reception about remembering to order more toilet paper and to check if they also needed a new supply of paper hand towels when her phone signalled an incoming call.

George saw her expression change as she glanced at the phone and said, 'Take it, I'll check everything and get an order in before I leave.'

A call from Ben already! She felt absurdly excited as she put her finger on the green button and put the phone to her ear, heading rapidly back to her office to be out of earshot for George, who was inquisitive and loved gossip.

'Are you busy? I can call later if you're in the middle of something.' Just hearing his voice made her smile. 'It's fine – you're not interrupting anything important, just a chat with our receptionist about ordering toilet paper.'

'I have an extra ticket to a show at the Little Angel tomorrow afternoon – would you like to come?'

'The puppet theatre? Are you into puppets?' She smiled at the image in her mind of Ben manipulating puppets; surely he was too large to have behind the scenes where room for the puppeteers must be limited.

'A reader gave me four tickets and I'm taking my nephew Squid, I mean Michael, and his little sister.

Their parents can't take them, but I thought you might like to come along.'

'I'd love to! I've never been there, but I have friends who say their kids love it. Why would someone who reads political columns give away tickets to a puppet theatre? Were they making fun of you?'

He chuckled. 'God no, it wasn't that kind of reader – it was someone who liked what I wrote in my other column about kids and screentime, the fun column. I'll text you the details and we'll meet at the theatre if that's OK with you.'

On Saturday afternoon, having braved the rain in a hooded jacket as she now had no umbrella, Amy stopped in the foyer of the theatre, pulled the wet hood off and shook her hair loose before she looked around for Ben. He'll be easy to spot in a crowd even for a short person, she thought and smiled to herself, like a lighthouse, or maybe a climbing wall, but he's not here yet. The thought of Ben as a climbing wall brough blush-making images into her head just as the smell of cinnamon swirled around her and was right behind her. 'There you are!'

When Ben introduced to Michael and Kayla she felt his focus on her like a nearly physical touch. She looked up from talking to the children and met his eyes and felt heat rise at the intensity of his gaze.

They sat with the children between them and passed the little program back and forth. 'I didn't realise that it was The Little Prince! I loved that book.' She turned from the program to the children. "Have you read it?'

Two heads shook a 'no' in unison, but Ben said, 'I've got a copy of it at my mum's place. I'll pick it up next time I see her and show you. I was fascinated by it as a boy – about your age, Michael.'

Amy looked at Micheal who was probably about the right age to appreciate "The Little Prince" in book form. 'The man who wrote it was a pilot and crashed in the desert. If you read it I'd like to hear what you think – maybe tastes have changed since I was a little girl.'

She caught a glance from Ben which confused her until she suddenly realised that what she had just said implied that she would be meeting them again. Today was obviously her day for blushing, that curse of the pale-skinned redhead. To avoid embarrassing herself further she turned her head and pretended to look at the children who has just arrived and sat down on her other side.

After ice creams and a short walk together they parted company. Ben and the children went one way and Amy set off home, alternating between thinking about those looks from Ben and the book she was writing, but unable to concentrate on either. She was no sooner inside the door than her phone buzzed in her pocket, so she pulled it out and took the call from Charlotte on speaker while trying to shrug out of her wet coat.

'What on earth are you doing? Are you in a fight?' Charlotte chuckled. 'It sounds weird.'

'Trying to take my sopping coat off without getting water on the phone,' said Amy and went to drop the coat in the bathroom. 'I just came in and I'm really wet. What are you up to?'

'I want some advice, or maybe I just need to talk through this with someone I trust, because I've got to make a decision based on practically nothing. It's about Breannah, she wants to meet with me – alone. Can you imagine? She just texted, but I haven't replied yet.'

'Who is Breannah? Oh, no – is she Roland's new woman? Why does she want to meet you alone?'

'She didn't say, and I don't want to reply or ask any questions until I've tried to figure out what this might be about. It's the strangest thing, isn't it?'

Amy found the whole situation very odd, but maybe it had something to do with the birthday party. Perhaps Breannah had said something that would give her a clue. 'Did you and her talk at the party? I haven't heard anything about how it went.'

'We did talk, but not one-on-one – it was a busy afternoon with all those kids and their parents. But as you said, a great way to meet her for the first time without too much tension. We probably exchanged five or six sentences in total, and they didn't stay long, an hour maybe. They left before the balloon man arrived.'

One mysterious thing after another, thought

Amy, and went to the kitchen to make a cup of coffee. 'Who's the balloon man?'

'That guy who comes to the kids' parties and makes animal shapes by twisting those long narrow ballons – you know! You must have seen them at markets and things.'

'Of course! And now Breannah wants to meet you – for coffee or what?'

'I'll read you the message, hang on - here it is. *Can we meet for coffee or a glass of wine, just the two of us. I think it might be useful, at least for me. Breannah.* That's all she says. She must have got my number from Roland's phone. At least for her – what could she possibly want from me that would be useful for her?'

Amy tried to imagine the consequences of Charlotte meeting with Breannah and could think of no reason why she shouldn't. 'I think you should meet her,' she said slowly. 'I mean, what could possibly happen? Nothing bad, at least not for you. If there *are* any repercussions they would land in her court - say if Roland discovers and has one of his angry fits. Just go and talk to her and find out what she wants.'

'OK, that's what I thought too, but I just wanted to check it with you before I replied. You're the only one of my friends I could ask. All the others would put too much convoluted speculation into it.'

'Great! And don't forget to let me know what happens – unless it's secret.' Amy ended the call and went to turn her laptop on, her mug of coffee beside her and an entire evening ahead with nobody but herself to please.

8

*S*unday morning and sunshine, bliss! thought Amy and watched the early morning sun cast a skewed rectangle of light on the wall opposite her bed, too relaxed to get up straight away to make a cup of coffee and a slice of toast to take back to bed as she usually did in the weekends. The previous night she had stayed up very late and written two chapters in the book she was now close to finishing, and the thought made her smile. The first draft was usually a mixture of intense satisfaction and slight frustration, like when a character refused to behave or talk the way she had intended and instead took on a life of their own, but stage two was pure fun. Reading through the entire story, slowly and steadily, and sometimes reading entire conversations out loud to herself, and then editing and adding and tweaking details to get it as perfect as she could. An enjoyable process and just as creative as making the story up from scratch.

And then stage three: loading it on her Kindle and reading it like a book written by someone else, an entirely different experience, but the process that made her notice things she had missed earlier.

Dreamily she stayed where she was and let random thoughts float through her mind, occasionally dwelling on the way Ben had looked at her the day before. She was brought back to reality by her phone buzzing quietly on the bedside table.

'Hi, I hope you were already awake,' said Kate cheerfully. 'Isn't it a great day after that deluge yesterday? I'm going to have lunch with some friends at the Southbank Centre food market first and then probably potter around the stalls. I thought you might like to join us.'

This needed no thought at all. 'I'd love to! What time will you be there?'

As soon as she ended the call with details organised of when and where to meet, Amy got up. When she set out for the Southbank Centre just before noon, she had managed to deal with some of the weekend tasks she had ignored the day before; the laundry was done, the flat had been sketchily vacuum cleaned and dusted, and the rest of day was now free to enjoy.

The lunch turned out to be unexpectedly entertaining, even though the three friends Kate was with had been strangers to Amy. A man and a woman, John and Gretchen, who Amy first assumed were a couple, but who turned out to be brother and sister, and another man who was the male sibling's partner. She smiled inside at her easy and totally wrong assumption of a conventional pairing. It's still kind of inbred, she thought, that male and female assumption, but maybe it was because of the way he had his arm around her shoulders when I walked up to them, such a couple type gesture.

Throughout lunch the four others debated one subject after another and Amy sat listening, mostly silently without making any contribution. They were obviously very good friends and had a kind of group alchemy that made it all right to be rudely ridiculing and to noisily debate minor points, ending in loud laughter. This was a side to Kate that she had never seen before and therefore as fascinating as it was surprising.

At one point the debate was about that Benson column Kate had mentioned some weeks ago, this time the subject had been "the horsey crowd" and much hilarity was aimed at Gretchen, who turned out to be an avid rider and spent a lot of time at some friend's place exercising their horses. 'Free labour,' said John's partner, whose name she hadn't caught. 'Equine exploitation.'

'Can you exploit someone who's willing – or more than willing – to do the work?' countered Kate. 'Surely not! If Gretchen wasn't invited to ride those horrid things every week, she'd probably be kneeling at the owners' feet begging to be allowed to ride them.'

'Of course I would, but luckily I don't have to. But I must say the Benson guy was a bit harsh in his descriptions of what he called the horsey crowd. My horsey people *do* have chins, and they don't say things that sound like old novels, like "I say, old chap" all the time.'

Amy took the opportunity to ask a few questions about the Benson column, but the opinions were divided. Kate thought it was mostly entertaining, but often harsh, as Gretchen had said, but both men thought it was hilarious.

'You can't seriously say he's hilarious all the time, though,' protested Kate. 'Sometimes I pity the people he makes fun of – just people doing their own thing and not trying to convert anyone else to whatever their hobbies or occupations are. They must feel the ridicule is personal sometimes.'

'I doubt it – he doesn't single out individuals, does he?' said the nameless man. 'Or very rarely. Mostly it's about groups, if you can call it that. Like the horse crowd.'

At the end of the afternoon Amy returned home with two carrier bags of products from the food market and a feeling of happy satisfaction. The entire weekend had been fun, despite yesterday's storm; puppet theatre, a gorgeous lunch in the sun with amusing company, a new side to Kate surprisingly revealed, and a lot of progress with her book. She put away her purchases and sat down at her laptop to read through yesterday's writing, but after only a few minutes she closed the document and googled "the Benson column".

What appeared was not a column written by someone with the surname Benson, it was Ben_son with an underscore in the middle and it was published each week in one of the major newspapers' weekend edition. Following a couple of links, she found the paper's archive of columns and started reading. Four issues back in time she had read only the first paragraph when she stopped as if frozen in place.

There was her author-name, the pseudonym she used for her light and frothy romantic novels, as far removed from her day-to-day job as one could imagine. Slowly she read his scathing little review, if that's what it was pretending to be and cringed with embarrassment, slammed the laptop lid down and got abruptly to her feet, angry and humiliated. There was no doubt in her mind that the writer was a male.

'That bastard,' she exclaimed furiously. 'That cheap shit - he gets a kick out of being nasty and making fun of people who do their best. And he's doing it for laughs, it's evil.'

It was definitely cruel and unnecessary, just as Kate had said, and being funny most of the time didn't make up for the casual nastiness. This must be one of those articles they had mentioned over lunch, where he picked on a named individual.

Amy poured herself a glass of wine and went to

sit on the balcony with a jacket over her shoulders. She had to admit that most men, and probably a lot of women too, would find her romance novels ridiculous or even laughable, nearly devoid of descriptive sex scenes and focused mainly on the sweet and funny rather than the hot and steamy.

Abstractedly gazing at the view through the glass balcony barrier she thought back to how cautious she had been at the outset, before she published her first novel on Amazon. She had changed her mind dozens of times about what name to adopt and nearly right away decided not to tell anyone at all, and now, of course, it was a blessing that she had kept it to herself. Thank goodness that Ben_son creep hadn't winkled out her real name, but he probably thought Julia Somerset was the writer's real name. She shuddered to think how it would have been now if she hadn't kept her writing and the pen name secret. Friends would read that column and comment, and worst of all, gossip about her. It would have been intolerable not to know who had read his scathing assessment, or who had told somebody else. She would have been forever wondering who knew and who didn't, and if people were laughing at her behind her back, and the thought made her cringe.

Over a dinner consisting of some of the luscious treats from the food market, she watched another episode of the Netflix series she'd started last week, but halfway through she paused it and sat rigid with the remote in her hand when a sudden insight struck her. Ben_son was Ben Anderson! Pete and Roger had mentioned he wrote a new column as well as his usual political one and so had Ben himself when he called about the puppet theatre. He said the tickets came from a reader of his "fun" column, not the political one. Amy sat staring at the muted TV screen, devastated and wished she could pretend it wasn't true, but it had to be, and it explained the underscore. He had used his first name and the last part of his surname as a pseudonym, which she had to admit was clever seeing he also wrote a serious political column, but what would happen now? He would have no idea that she was Julia Somerset, but that changed nothing about the effect it had on her. The scorn and ridicule he had heaped on romance writers, using her as an example, was like a slap in the face.

9

Over dinner with Patrick the following week, once again at his favourite and very expensive restaurant where they were now eating for the third time, Amy decided to ask a few questions.

'I've been reading up on low testosterone and the effect it has on a man.' She paused and looked carefully at Patrick. 'I hope you don't mind talking about it, but it's very interesting and for once we have a table when nobody can overhear us, at least if we speak reasonably quietly. Some of the things I've read indicate that very low testosterone levels also mean low bone mass end low muscle mass. But you have the physique of the perfect male – I could feel the muscles when you hugged me just now. Is there some explanation for this?'

'No, nobody has a clue. Over the last few years I've been written up in three or four articles by researchers, who study this particular subject. You wouldn't believe how many blood samples I've been subjected to, probably hundreds.' He gave her a wry smile. 'Apparently I'm unique. The lack of libido is obviously due to low testosterone and so far I'm quite content not to take supplements – you can't miss what you've never had, can you? I feel as if my physical make-up is who I am, and I don't want to change it, there's not need.' He looked carefully at her to gauge her reaction. 'I know it sounds crazy, but I'm used to having no sex drive and I'm happy as I am. But nobody can explain why I have the physique I have, that's what intrigues the experts.'

'Don't you feel you're missing out? But I suppose you can change your mind about the testosterone supplements at any time.'

'I tried to explain it to my doctor a while back. I said I feel as if my whole personality might change if I take the drug – I've got this weird feeling that I'm complete like this, and I don't want to rock the boat. It sounds insane, but it's a strong feeling.'

'I think I can understand that. Not that I've got anything to compare it to, but if it's a strong feeling, why would you do it? But tell me more,' said Amy and took a sip of her wine while she studied him over the rim of the glass. 'If you don't mind, but I find it fascinating - I love science. You're every woman's dream man, apart from the fact that you're not interested in sex. You defy the hormonal laws, *and* you don't seem to mind any of it. And women are obviously attracted to you, I can see it every time we walk into a bar or a restaurant - those lustful looks! What do they mean to you apart from being good for your ego and your job?'

Patrick lifted his glass in a toast. 'I don't mind talking about it and you don't seem to mind how weird I am – you're such a bonus in my life, Amy. But there's really very little to tell. I have quite a few women friends, and you've become my best friend, because I can talk to you about something I normally keep very quiet. So, here's how it is - when a woman tries to get me into bed, I have to make a decision based on two things. Do I feel it's worth the effort to try to have sex with her, which can be a struggle, usually is - or do I trust her enough to tell her the truth? And the answer to both those questions is nearly invariably "no". I usually say I don't fancy her that way, but I like her a lot, and mostly I get away with it without any major drama.'

'But sometimes you end up in some kind of argument? Some woman has a hissy-fit because she's been turned down?'

Two creases appeared between Patrick's perfectly groomed dark eyebrows and now he looked sad. 'Yeah, you're right, that does happen. And that's why it's so precious when I find a woman like you, who can accept me for what I am and not make any demands.' He gave her a wicked grin. 'And at the same time enhance my reputation by being seen with me.'

'Oh, for God's sake! Don't make me out to be some kind of saint. I'm not going out with you out of the goodness of my heart like some kind of charity act. I love being taken to good restaurants, and I like talking to you even if you don't read books, so let's just keep going out now and then. And I'm getting very fond of you.' She laughed quietly. 'It's a bit like having a brother – which I've never had. I haven't had a man friend for quite a while and going out alone to a restaurant is no fun. I usually go to cafes and bistros with my women friends and sometimes with my dad. This is a real treat.'

On the way home on the tube Amy thought back over the conversation they had had in the restaurant and tried to put herself in Patrick's place. She wondered if he sometimes fell in love with someone in a romantic way, and if he did, would it be a sexless romance? How likely was it that he'd form a romantic attachment to someone, who was also asexual? The subject might lend itself to a book, but very different from the normal romance template – something more serious, but possibly a theme she could build on and develop. Maybe an asexual man falling in love with an asexual woman? And would it be easier for an asexual woman to reach sexual satisfaction even if she lacked libido? She must ask him if there were interest groups online for asexual people where they could find and date each other. That Patrick was happy and well-balanced was obvious, but did he envy other men? He had said he didn't miss the things he might have experienced if he wasn't asexual, that he didn't miss what he didn't have, but maybe that was just his way of not having to talk about feelings he kept to himself?' After a moment she realised that couldn't be it. If that was all it was he would take the supplement and change.

She thought back to how dismissive she had been when she first met him. How his vanity and the lack of shared interests made her feel he was shallow or even slightly ridiculous. But now that she knew him so much better and understood his problem, she had become very fond of him. He was kind and generous and didn't seem to resent his rather strange condition, and he wasn't bitter or envious of others. He had become a close and precious friend whose secrets and interests she would safeguard.

10

Since she arranged the date Amy had several times decided that her re-education plan for Ben was a bad idea, and she should just cancel the date and never see him again. It was all very well to plan a campaign to educate him about his lack of consideration and empathy, but despite telling herself that she could contain her feelings and be sensible, a slight worry hovered in the back of her mind that maybe dating him at all might be a mistake. Potentially a huge mistake, she thought, as she brushed her hair and picked up her bag on the Saturday morning, but she suppressed the thought – she was determined to see this through, and she was ready.

Exiting the tube at the Lancaster Gate Amy set out across Hyde Park with indecision still tormenting her despite how many times she had told herself she could do this without getting too emotionally involved and possibly destroyed. She usually took this route to the Victoria & Albert Museum even though it was a far longer walk compared to exiting at the South Kensington station, but she loved walking across Hyde Park and then down Exhibition Road. Today she nearly stopped by the Long Water to text Ben and cancel their date. She could find some other way to deal with him without risk to herself, but somehow she found herself walking around the corner into Cromwell Road without having sent that message, and then it was too late to turn around. The thought of him watching her turn and walk back the way she had come was too much to contemplate, and it would inevitably involve her in an exchange of text messages with questions and excuses, and it wasn't as if she wasn't brave enough to front up to him. Not that he knew what she was planning, but he might think she had second thoughts because she didn't like him enough. And then she cringed at the idea that she cared enough about him to feel she mustn't hurt him. What was wrong with her? For a usually decisive person she was behaving very out of character.

Standing by the main entrance to the museum she saw him approach before he had noticed her. Now it starts, she thought and subconsciously pulled her shoulders back, now she must watch what she said and did, and make sure she got this right. Her feelings about him must be ignored and consigned to some remote storage place in her mind where they would cease to torment her.

'Amy, hi! What an unusual place for a date! But I've known since the moment I met you that you're possibly unique. Are we looking at an exhibition here first or is there a cafe or a restaurant inside?'

She couldn't help smiling. He was that kind of man; if he smiled you simply found yourself smiling back. But being friendly was part of the plan, so what caused the smile was irrelevant. 'Have you never been here before?'

'I've walked past a few times,' he said casually. 'Usually on my way to or from the Natural History Museum next-door, where I take Michael now and then – he loves the place, but I've never been tempted to go inside this one. Does it have some sort of significance for you?'

She led the way up the steps and said over her shoulder, 'You just wait! This place is full of surprises, and it's become my favourite place to have coffee or lunch ever since my friend Kate introduced me to it. And like all museums these days, they make you either enter or exit through the gift shop, which is a very clever idea.' She was rewarded by a chuckle from Ben and smiled to herself.

They walked side by side across the sculpture gallery and she noticed him looking in both directions, taking in the length of the gallery, but she carried on around the corner of the courtyard garden and sensed his slight change of direction when he spotted the garden café. 'No, not that one, we'll continue around the next corner.'

When they entered the Gamble room Ben stopped abruptly just inside the door. The expression on his face as he looked around made her laugh, because this was obviously not what he had expected. 'Good Lord – what a magnificent place! I can't believe I never heard of it before.'

Amy felt as if she had created the room herself, her pleasure in revealing it to someone else was intense. 'Isn't it splendid?'

They remained where they were for a couple of minutes while Ben silently studied the extravagant, glittering room. They got a table just where Amy most liked to sit. 'I love sitting by these pillars.' She looked up at the one closest to their table. 'Aren't they fabulous? This interior it's like a treasure chest - like opening a jewellery box and climbing right in.'

Ben tilted his head back to look up at the ceiling high above them. 'Look at that! It's not just the way it's painted - it's 3D too, embossed. I wonder how they did that? This was built in the nineteenth century, wasn't it? And there were no scissor lifts in those days – they must have lain on their backs on scaffolding like Michel Angelo in the Sistine chapel.'

Amy knew it was unreasonable to feel so pleased that he liked the place, but a shared delight always did that to her. Finding someone else who loved the things she did was something to be treasured.

'I researched it after the first time I came. The ceiling is made of thin sheets of iron pressed in moulds and then painted on the ground before they lifted them – however they did that – loads of scaffolding, I imagine. And all the glittering mosaic and gilding, the little reflections coming at you from all directions – it just makes me smile.'

Ben chuckled again, and she smiled at his pleasure. 'And guess what? This was the first museum in England with gas lighting *and* the first with a restaurant, so it's truly special. Not only gorgeous and glittering, but part of London history in more ways than one.'

Now he did laugh. 'You're one out of the box, like my grandma used to say. What with this and that fork of yours – the discipline fork!'

This was a chance, the perfect opportunity that she had thought she might have to manufacture, but here it was just appearing out of nowhere. 'So, none of the people you make fun of in your Ben_son column approach you with a discipline fork?'

'God, no,' he said, casually dismissing the idea. 'I think everyone understands it's just fun, it's not personal. That column is light entertainment, pure and simple. Such a nice change from politics.'

Ah, she thought, so he's never thought about it from the victim's point of view, it's all about the fun he gets out of composing his sarcastic comments.

'Are you sure people understand that? I went back and read a few after I met you at Pete's. I wasn't aware of your column until then, but I must say I did wonder how people feel when you mock them. You're extremely good at making sarcastic fun of people and their various life choices, but don't you ever wonder how hurt they might feel?'

He looked at her as if she had completely missed the point of what he had already said. 'It's just entertainment, Amy. I've never had anyone have a go at me or complain to the paper - not once.'

'But maybe they wouldn't have a go at you,' she said and tried to keep her voice casual and reasonably light-hearted. 'Maybe people don't know *how* to do it. It's not as if you write under your real name, is it?'

'OK, give me an example.' He sounded as if was indulging her. 'Tell me something I wrote that someone might feel really upset about.'

She pretended to think. The way she would phrase this was clear in her mind, but she wanted him to think that she was pondering his question and took her time. 'I know - what about the piece you wrote about that romance writer - Julia somebody. That was pretty cutting, and it named her, made it personal.' Not cutting, she thought, eviscerating is a better word, gut-wrenchingly hurtful and belittling.

He made a dismissive gesture and casually took a sip of his wine before he replied. 'I don't think she'd take it personally. I'm sure Julia whatever-her-name-was knew I was taking a poke at the romance writing industry as such, not at her personally.'

'You were pretty scathing - I think she would have felt humiliated. You named and shamed her, after all. It must have felt personal to her.' Don't get too heated, Amy silently warned herself, don't lose the plot.

'I hope you don't expect me to apologise in next week's column.' He grinned, and she could tell that her concern had not registered on any deep level, or any level at all. She would have to be careful around him, she found him very sexy in a large and solid way. She mustn't get too attached, or she would end up hurt, because if gentle re-education didn't work, the end game would be to take him down a peg or two, preferably publicly. But only if the personal approach didn't work. And then their little dating relationship would be over, and any future developments obliterated.

They shared the bill again, because no way was she going to let him pay for her when she was plotting to teach him a lesson, but all she said was, 'I never let a guy pay for me on the first few dates – and sometimes never. What if I decide I hate him by date six and want to stab him with my fork? It just wouldn't feel right if he'd paid for my lunch.'

They were walking across Hyde Park with no particular goal in mind when Ben suddenly grabbed her arm and swung her to one side, then stepped in front of her, taking her so completely by surprise that she nearly fell over. The large Pitbull terrier cross, which had come hurtling towards them with its lead flying behind, was now right in front of Ben's legs, but it wasn't in attack mode. Its rear end wagged in ecstasy, and within a few seconds the owner caught up, panting and apologetic after a fast run. 'Oh God, I'm so sorry! I don't know why she does this, but every time she sees a large man - and I don't mean fat, I mean just big, like you - she tries to pull me towards them. This time I wasn't prepared, so I lost my grip on her lead.'

'Oh, I'm used to it,' said Ben easily and bent to rub the dog's ears. 'It happens all the time - women and dogs come hurtling towards me.'

The woman laughed and after another apology she walked away with her dog looking longingly back at Ben.

'That was a fast save! If that dog *had* been set on taking a bite out of someone, it would have been out of you.'

'But I couldn't let a dog take a bite out of a woman who looks like you, could I? What if it had ruined your chances as a model? But I hope I didn't hurt you when I pushed you. People tell me I don't know my own strength, but I had to do it fast to get you out of the way.'

11

When the courier bag from New Zealand arrived at the office, her first thought was that she would keep it and open it at home that night. She tucked it into her bag and carried on with the cashflow analysis in a bankruptcy she was investigating for an insurance fraud case, but within ten minutes her curiosity got the better of her and she pulled it out again. In the courier bag was a perfectly ordinary white envelope and holding it made her feel a mixture of dread and excitement. Inside that envelope was something her mother had felt was important enough to make sure she received, possibly something nobody else knew, but which her mother felt Amy should know, or it might be advice about life which she would no longer be around to give her. It had to be something significant, or why had her mother gone to the trouble to write the letter and then send it to her sister in another country and ask her to keep it for such a specific length of time.

Though Amy had no direct memories of her mother, she sometimes felt as if she did. Her father had told her stories about how they had met as teenagers, about their wedding and about her own first years, but Amy had always felt that her memories were indirect, simply planted in her mind by what her father told her and photographs she had seen of her mother and herself. But now she was about to read something her mother had written, to see her words in her own handwriting, which felt exciting and ominous in equal measure. She tried to remember if she had ever seen an example of her handwriting and decided she hadn't. She imagined her mother sitting at a table considering how to phrase whatever it was she was going to write. Amy's mind drifted through these thoughts and circled back to Aunt Susie's letter, and how she had emphasised that she had no idea what the contents might be.

When she finally snapped back to the present she pulled on the envelope flap, and it popped open with a little crackling sound of adhesive that had dried after so many years. The letter contained two pages that looked as if they had been pulled out of a school exercise book, closely ruled pages filled from top to bottom on both sides with tiny handwriting. She read the letter right through very quickly, eager to get to the point, then she put the paper down on her desk and turned the chair around to stare out the window in stunned disbelief. Whatever she had expected this could have been further from her mind. She had speculated about the letter ever since Susie contacted her and decided that the most likely thing was life advice or family history, but what she had just read was like bolt of lightning from a clear sky.

After a few minutes of silent contemplation Amy swung back to her desk, picked the letter up again and re-read it very slowly to make sure no implications were missed.

Darling Amy, I send this letter to Susie for her to keep until you turn thirty. I want you to know something that nobody else knows, and I want you to consider carefully how it would impact on your father if you tell him. What I'm going to tell you I have kept to myself and never mentioned to a living soul, your father has no idea. Two years after we got married I got pregnant with you and here is the secret only you will know once I am dead - I think you were fathered by my lover. I know this is a disturbing thing to tell you, but I feel you should know. I hope it will not damage your relationship with your dad, but it might very well change how you look at me as a person. I hope you won't judge me too harshly when I tell you how this brief affair developed and ended. At the time your dad was building his antique business and spent long hours in the shop in the evenings, cleaning and fixing things, painting the walls, building shelves and trying to create the kind of environment he wanted to display his goods in. He was often away in the weekends attending house sales and auctions that had been advertised, and sometimes he closed the shop and was away for three or four weekdays and managed to cover several events in a couple of towns in some part of the country. He would come back with the station wagon loaded with small items and bigger things would arrive in the following days by truck. The law office where I worked as a clerk was large with many employees and six partners, and the Friday night drinks at the pub around the corner was a standing event. I can't explain why I did it, because I wasn't bored and I loved your father, but for some reason I entered into a brief relationship with one of the partners – flattering attention and lust, I think. It only lasted a couple of months before I broke it off, when I suddenly came to my senses and realised that I was risking everything for a short term thrill. I left my job after realising I was pregnant. There might be things in your personality or appearance that seem out of context – your mane of red hair has been commented on since you were a year old, and we say we have no idea where it came from, but there must have been someone in our past with hair like yours, maybe a Viking ancestor in your dad's past. I'm nearly certain your biological father is the man I had the affair with. I never mentioned a word about this to anyone, not to my best friend, or my sister or your father. Always remember that you are the best and most precious thing in my life. Mum

Talk about shockwaves, thought Amy as she slowly folded the letter to put it back in the envelope. But why didn't she tell me the name of her lover, and why tell me at all? Without a name it means nothing, but perhaps she wasn't thinking clearly. She would have been in her final round of treatment when she wrote this. Or was she worried I might find my biological father and confront him? Did she think it would change my relationship with my dad if I did find him?

She put the envelope in her bag and tried to concentrate on what was on her screen, but the large spreadsheet with data that she had exported from the bank failed to hold her attention. She closed it down, picked up her bag and left an hour earlier than she normally would.

my could find nothing that seemed interesting either amongst her books or on TV, and she was stuck with a plot problem in the book she was writing. But when she watched the news that evening the acronym DNA popped up in an interview and gave her an idea. She had known for several years that her father had had his DNA tested, and at the time he had suggested that she do it too, a suggestion she had rejected out of hand as uninteresting and unnecessary. She said she already knew a lot about her mother's side of the family, and he could tell her what he found about his own ancestry, and he admitted it was probably pointless. At the time he didn't press the point, and only later would she wonder why he hadn't stressed that she might find more maternal connections than she was aware of. When she asked him why he had his own DNA done at all, he said he thought it would be interesting to see how many relatives he had in other parts of the country, aside from those he had always known about in the area he came from in Nottinghamshire.

But if she had her DNA analysed now it would give her an insight into whose daughter she was, confirm if she was not the child of the man she had always thought was her father and maybe find out who her mother's lover was. She could tick the box her father had told her about to allow the DNA company to advise her of any close relatives the test linked her directly to, and then she would know.

Naturally she wouldn't tell him that she had done it, so if it turned out he was not her biological father it would not seem odd that the link had not come up in his data. Not that it mattered in any real way; he was her dad, and that was all there was to it, and whatever biology or genetics came up with would make no difference to their relationship, at least from her point of view. But it would be a shock for him to find his wife had cheated on him, something she definitely didn't want to happen, so she would say nothing. If he was her biological father, she would pop up in a notification to him, and she would say that, yes, she had done the test after all. But it would be interesting to see what close relationships the analysis brought up, a little journey of stealthy detective work and possible discovery.

She turned the TV off and flicked up the lid up on her laptop, hoping she would be able to identify the company her father had mentioned. Or maybe it didn't have to be the same company, she thought. Perhaps they all used data from some central DNA database and added new data as it came in? Like a whole-world depository of human genetics. She ordered a test kit and felt quite energized by this sudden decision, went back to the stalled manuscript and wrote another two thousand words, inspired and happy. When she finally went to bed it was very late, but sleep evaded her, and she lay awake speculating on what the rest results might reveal. She wondered how she would feel if she discovered she had siblings, or rather half siblings, whom she had never heard about, and whether she would be tempted to make contact with them. When she woke the next morning she felt she had put a problematic decision behind her and got up with a feeling of relief, as if whatever the outcome it would be better than not knowing.

Not until several days later when the test kit had arrived, her inside cheek had been swabbed and the little parcel returned to the company, did she think of the possibility that those potential half siblings might make contact with her whether she wanted it or not. They would be told her name and age and which country she lived in, so they might find her. She tried to put it out of her mind as something relatively unimportant, which she had done mostly out of idle curiosity, but now the thought of what might result from the test lurked in the back of her mind like a vague threat, a hint of potential consequences she should have considered earlier.

The feeling stayed with her right through what turned into a fraught Friday at work when the new recruit tested her patience with a display of unexpected argumentativeness, and the background buzz in her head made her show her impatience. At the end of the afternoon her conscience got the better of her and she walked down the corridor to his room.

'I'm sorry I was so irritable earlier,' she said and hoped he wouldn't be embarrassed, even though the incident had been mostly his doing. 'I've had a minor worry on my mind all day and it made me short tempered – not how I usually behave.'

Grant looked first surprised and then he grinned. 'I deserved it – such a stupid mistake to have made, and then I argued about it! I think in general you're the most patient person I've ever met – and I've tested that patience now and then, I know that.'

'Well, then I can only hope you never get to see me having a tantrum! I do have a temper to match my hair, you know, but I've learnt to mostly control it.' They both laughed and she knew they had reached a new level of understanding.

The next day Amy and Kate met for lunch at the V&A again, and, as topics sometimes mysteriously do, DNA came up in the conversation at an early stage.

'I'll tell you what happened today,' said Kate and

sounded quite excited. 'This morning, I got an e-mail about my DNA test. Well, not about the test as such, but I got a notification that they've found what they call a new connection. I've had lots before but nothing as interesting or as closely related as this one - it turns out I have a first cousin on my mother's side living in England. Which is kind of crazy, because my mama came here from France when she married my dad, and I didn't think I had any relations at all from her side living in England.'

To Amy this revelation was such a coincidence that for a moment she struggled to reply while she internally debated whether she would tell Kate about the letter and her own DNA test. To gain time she pushed the thought aside and said, 'I didn't know you were half French! Why on earth did you never tell me?'

Kate looked slightly confused at this exclamation. 'Why would I tell you unless it came up in some other context? I mean, your mother might have been Russian or Greek. Would you have mentioned it right out of context?'

'I don't know, but I think it's *very* interesting. And now that I know, I think it explains a couple of things about you - things that are characteristic of you, of your personality. I bet it comes from the French side.'

'What on earth are you talking about? What is it about me that you think is explained by my French blood?' Kate was looking as if she was about to burst into laughter, she had that "trying to look serious" face she often adopted, but the corners of her mouth were tweaking up.

'Your fashion sense for a start - not necessarily how you dress yourself, which seems more like disguise than anything else, but things you have sometimes hinted at to me. Like that time at the beginning of the summer when you casually mentioned dark aubergine, - and you were so right! I bought a dress in just that colour and I it's my favourite dress now. The colour does something amazing for my hair and skin, just as you said. And it's not the first time you've done it either.' Amy paused and thought for a moment. 'And remember when my ex-partner Simon tried to hassle me, right here - I think we were at this same table? And you put him in his place so effectively! Probably something a French woman would do, not quite how any of my other friends would have dared tackle him.'

Shaking her head as if she couldn't believe what she heard, Kate studied Amy for a moment as if she was making sure she wasn't joking. 'Sometimes you're so funny, Amy! I never know what you're going to say next. I don't think those things have anything to do with being half French. But back to this unknown cousin - don't you think it's amazing to find someone so closely related that you've never heard of?'

She looked a question at Amy, who could think of nothing to say. 'I think it's a cousin from an affair my mother's brother must have had. He lived in

Bristol for a year or two when he was young, played football for some county team or something.'

Amy considered for a moment and tried to imagine how she herself would react if, or perhaps when a sibling, who was also a stranger, would contact her. But for the moment she wouldn't tell anyone about either the letter from her mother or her own DNA test, so all she said was, 'Or maybe it's someone who moved here from France. Oh no, then you'd know about her already, of course. Maybe your uncle did have a baby with someone? And if he did, he obviously didn't tell anyone, or you'd have known – or maybe he never knew he fathered a half English child.'

'Well, I don't have a clue,' said Kate cheerfully, 'but there's always a chance that *I'm* the one who was adopted. I'd never really thought of it before, but I'm not in the least like anyone else in the family. My three siblings are tall and slender with blondish hair just like my dad. And my mum wasn't built like a pumpkin either, so I'm the family anomaly. But then my DNA wouldn't have linked me to known relatives, of course. No, silly thinking, I can't be adopted – though admit it's an intriguing thought to have at my age.'

Amy frowned at this latest piece of self-deprecation. 'Please don't call yourself a pumpkin, Kate! You're not a pumpkin, you're just nicely rounded.'

Seemingly unconcerned, Kate just smiled, but it was hard to tell how genuine her amusement was.

'But I'm also very short, which means that being nicely rounded makes me nearly as wide as I'm tall. But let's say I'm a butterball then, if you object to likening me to a pumpkin.'

This conversation was very interesting because here right in front of Amy was a person, who was in a situation where she had to make a choice about whether to contact someone who was a new connection in the family, or not. 'Are you going to get in touch with the mystery cousin?'

'Probably,' said Kate and swiped her finger over her phone. 'Or she might get in touch with me. I'm just looking her up again so I can tell you her name. Ah, here it is. Her name is Jennifer Blackett - unusual surname. I don't think I've ever met anyone called Blackett.'

They talked about other things while they ate their lunch and as always, they compared their dishes and decided who had made the best choice.

'Nothing, but nothing can beat a fresh bagel with salmon and cream cheese!' Amy cut a piece off her bagel, speared it on her fork and held it out across the table. 'Just taste this! The bagels here are the best I've ever had.'

'Very nice but brace yourself for this!' Kate lifted her fork loaded with fabada, which seemed to be one of her favourite food choices. 'I know you've tasted this before, but it's particularly good today.'

With the food tasting over they did what they usually did, talked about what they were reading, what foolish or outrageous things politicians on both sides of the House had said or done, and finally got back to the unknown cousin. 'Promise you'll tell me if you get in touch with her,' said Amy when they parted. 'I'm dying to hear the background – it's like something out of a novel, maybe one by Kate Atkinson.'

13

As time went by Amy realised that she was falling deeply in love with Ben, but her re-education plan, potentially to turn into a revenge plan, remained unchanged in her mind. She knew she was taking an emotional risk, and she would regret losing him when she finally reached the end of her campaign, unless she could make him understand how deeply he hurt people sometimes. It wasn't an outcome she had taken seriously enough at the beginning, when she just felt vaguely attracted, but things had changed, and now she was forced to admit that when she did drop him, or more likely when he dropped her, she would be devastated. Occasionally, when she woke in the night, she wondered if she shouldn't just give up on the whole idea and simply enjoy being with him, her cinnamon man, the only one she had ever come across. But despite this invisible scent link, they had no real long-term future if he couldn't be brought to understand how damaging his sarcastic humour could be. And if he was unable to see it, then they definitely had no future because to her the idea of callous disregard for those he identified as individuals, was incomprehensible.

But the knowledge that he would learn nothing, if she didn't go through to the bitter end, made it impossible to back away from her plan. There just had to be enough compassion in him to understand her concern. Now and again, she sat down and tried to work out the best wording for the comment she would compile and upload on the paper's online Reader's Notes page, if all else failed. Now that she had studied that page for a few weeks she realised how powerful it was. Readers responded to the comments of others, and it generated discussions, not only on the Readers' page but also in social media, particularly Instagram. She had tracked some topics and was beginning to see how she could make her own comment work most effectively, get traction in other media and possibly make the issue take on a life of its own.

Imagine, she thought, if it becomes a meme all over the online world. And hot on the heels of that idea came the thought of how this would feel for Ben. Very harsh and punitive, and what if it still didn't change his perceptions of what was humour and what was hurtful?

After thinking about this for a few days and imagining how painful it would be for him, she mentally changed tacks and decided to make her reader comment more moderate. It wasn't wimping out, she told herself during these internal midnight debates, it was just being more careful about people's feelings than he was.

As Amy gradually fell deeper in love, she began to wonder if she was going to have to leap on him, knock him to the ground and ravish him. He had made no suggestions about a late drink at her place after a meal out, or that she should come and see where he lived, the kind of suggestions that would normally indicate that someone wanted to take her to bed. She knew he was deeply attracted, there was no doubt in her mind. That fizzing tingle when he touched her, as he often did, was definitely mutual, and the way he looked so intently at her sometimes. She could sense his reaction when he hugged her, kissed her cheek or touched her hand.

By their sixth date she found herself so looking forward to seeing him that her heart leapt in her chest when she saw him coming towards her outside the V&A, where they were meeting for lunch again. This time he didn't just kiss her cheek, he pulled her into a tight hug and said, '*There* you are!' as if he hadn't seen her for weeks, or maybe as if he hadn't expected her to turn up. She relished the feel of being held so closely and leaned into him for a moment. Then he pushed her slightly away and smiled. 'I think I'm becoming fond of this place. It feels like it's our special place.'

'It's definitely my special place - this is where I meet my friend Kate for lunch or coffee, and she gives me all kinds of advice, all of which is really good. She's an amazing woman.'

'What kind of advice?' asked Ben as they walked into the cafe. 'About your love life or what?'

'All kinds of things.' It made Amy laugh to think of the variety of topics where Kate's advice had been invaluable. 'She once got rid of a man who came up to our table, someone I really didn't want to see, a guy who was pestering me. And if you could have seen her, five foot nothing and quite chubby but also gorgeous, telling a very up-himself tall man where to get off - you would have laughed. But aside from that she's good with fashion advice and she recommends really good books.'

They were halfway through lunch and had just decided to have as second glass of wine each, when he surprised her and brought up her initial query from their first date about how people responded to being mocked in public, possibly reminded by her mentioning Kate's book recommendations.

He looked at her in a slightly hesitant way across the table. 'You know how you mentioned that column I'd written - the first time we went out? The one about the romance writer. What was it in that story you objected to? I'd be interested to hear what it was because it seemed to me as if you were particularly upset about it. I could sense that it had stuck in your mind for some reason.'

'I'd have to go back the article,' said Amy and tried to sound slightly confused as if she couldn't remember exactly what it was. 'I can't recall the details now. I do remember the romance writer, but not exactly what you wrote about her – just that I thought it must have been humiliating for her to read it.' Which was a lie of course, as the exact phrases were etched on her brain and would probably remain there forever.

Ben got his phone out and passed it across the table, and she realised that it wasn't her mention of Kate that had reminded him. He had been thinking about this already. 'This is the column in question. I pulled it up before I came because I really wanted to ask you about this. I remember we had quite a little discussion about it.'

'Let me see,' said Amy and took the phone. 'Oh yes, I remember now.' She read out the paragraph that had made her get up from the table in tears when she first read it in her own flat.

'Julia Somerset's novels are the perfect example: romantic drivel, fanciful emotional nonsense, written to make women without a man in their lives feel good, to make them believe that sooner or later true love will come their way, complete with handsome hero and the trite and nauseating happy-ever-after ending. Or maybe it's for women who no longer get any pleasure out of their relationship? But is it helpful to spread this romance rubbish? It's formulaic and insulting to the rational mind, only read by women, and it contributes nothing to human understanding or progress. Julia constructs the prescribed unlikely pairing, introduces far-fetched misunderstandings, overheard comments and passionate, smouldering looks as per the accepted formula. Then

comes the reconciliation after endless pages of self-doubt, repetitive musings on what was said or not said, and then the touching ending where true love triumphs. Sick-making drivel – or do you like it? And if so, are you game enough to admit you like it? Would you explain it to me? They say most women read romance as light relief - but relief from what?

She handed the phone back and tried to give him a casual smile, but it felt more like a grimace. 'I remember now - I objected to how dismissive you were of something that provides a distraction in other people's lives. Harmless, happy stories, sometimes with an element of light porn and sometimes the kind that, as they say, stops at the bedroom door or not far beyond it. I read one of her books right through after reading that particular column of yours, and I could see no harm in it.'

'But admit it's rubbish,' said Ben and smiled with his eyes creasing at the outer corners in that endearing way that she had come to love. 'It might be harmless, but does it have any value? Does it make anything think? Does it add anything to anyone's life apart from a passing distraction?'

Amy looked straight into his eyes, without a smile to soften what she was going to say, her predetermined statement. 'And do you think your sarcastic evaluation of romance novels adds anything to anyone's life? It might just detract from quite a few people's lives. Both those who enjoy that kind of book and those who write them. They probably felt belittled or even humiliated after reading your column.'

He looked thoughtful, but only for a moment, but then he smiled. 'Surely not! The column isn't intended to be more than just fun. I don't aim to add anything of value to humanity, all I do is entertain and amuse, though that time I was probably a bit harsh – not my usual style. I admit I shouldn't have made that comment about adding lasting value - I have no pretensions of lasting value when it comes to my own writing.'

'Just like the romance writers, they don't make any claims of lasting value either. The only real difference is that you potentially upset and hurt people, and she doesn't.'

Awkwardly they changed the subject and talked of other things, and Amy wondered if he had understood what she was trying to put across, because she couldn't make it any clearer - that there was really very little difference between what motivated her to write the sort of books she wrote, and what motivated him to write his Ben_son column, though at least her own writing never insulted or hurt anyone.

For some perverse reason, she suddenly felt that this was the day when she had to get him into bed, which seemed strange considering their conversation, but maybe it was because she knew now that very soon this would be over, and she would probably never see him again. The thought that this could not possibly end well had grown in her mind over the last week until it had become a conviction, and today's conversation had proved her right.

They went for their customary walk across Hyde Park and halfway to the Bayswater tube station, she took his hand. 'Would you like to go to bed with me? I've been wanting to ask you since our second date, but I suppose I was doing that ridiculous female romance-novel-induced thing of waiting for you to ask me.'

'I can't think of anything I would like more. Believe it or not, I was just about to suggest the same thing.'

As soon as they were inside her door Ben took his jacket off, threw it on a chair and said, 'Where's the bedroom?' and Amy dropped her bag and coat on the floor and pointed. Before she knew what was happening Ben had picked her up in his arms and was walking through the door to her bedroom. She just had time to be impressed by his strength before he tipped her off on to the bed.

'Look at you, you gorgeous thing.' He leaned over her with his hands each side of her shoulders and smiled before he briefly kissed her and straightened up. 'Am I going to be allowed to undress you?'

Very gently he raised her into a sitting position and peeled her top off the way you undress a small child, one sleeve at a time then over her head. When she was naked on the bed he knelt beside the bed and ran one hand slowly down her body from her shoulder to her hip. 'This seems unreal – I never thought this would happen. Somehow I kept getting little vibes of dislike from you now and then, which was puzzling, so I wasn't expecting you to suggest this.'

He got out of his clothes and Amy watched as the size and strength of him was revealed and registered how wrong she had been about his bulk. She had never realised anyone could be that large without quite a lot of it being fat, but clearly it was just the muscle mass based on a large bone structure. Ben got onto the bed beside her and lay propped up on one elbow looking down into her face. His hand once again stroked her from shoulder to hip and the slowly back.

Amy was nearly purring now, she put her hand on his and said, 'This feels so good. I love your hands.'

Some time later she came back to earth after a touch sensation like she had never before experienced. 'That was amazing!' She rolled over on top of him and rested her forearms on his chest looking down into his eyes and her hair hung like a red curtain around their faces. 'What would you like me to do to you?'

'Anything - whatever you like.' He chuckled. 'I'm your playground, but if you wriggle like that it will be over very quickly.'

They spent the whole afternoon in bed, lying

face to face talking, and as the late sun left the bedroom and the sense of day's end filtered in, they made love again, and she knew she would not be able to carry out her revenge plan. She could no longer contemplate alienating and losing him, and if she couldn't change him she would have to learn to live with his occasionally hurtful, sarcastic wit.

14

*L*ate one evening the following week when Amy was about to turn off her laptop, an email from the DNA company pinged into her Inbox with a message headed "We have connections for you!"

For a moment she considered turning the laptop off and looking at it later. The prospect of being told she had half siblings was not one to take lightly, and now she suddenly realised that it was an imminent possibility. What if they wanted to meet her when they were told they had a half-sister they had never known about? But then rational thought slid quickly back into her mind, as it usually did after a moment of panic or uncertainty. Looking at the message right now or later would change nothing. Even if she never looked at it at all, there was still the possibility that an unknown half-sibling would find her or simply ask the DNA company's website to make contact, so she opened the message.

We have found three close connections:

Delia Wilson, probably half-sister, 42 years old – 97% certainty. This person does not want to be contacted."

Jonathon Wilson, probably half-brother, 46 years old – 97% certainty. This person may be contacted."

Frank Wilson, parent, 76 years old – 99% certainty. This person may be contacted.

Amy got to her feet and stood staring at the screen with her arms wrapped around her middle, feeling suddenly cold and shivery. She wished she had read the instructions a bit more closely and really considered the possible consequences when she set up her DNA account, because now she couldn't remember if she had ticked the box that she could be contacted. Maybe that wording "this person may be contacted" indicated that they had ticked that box, but she hadn't, so it was up to her to either contact them or not. She considered this for a few moments and decided that was probably the most logical explanation. Presumably on that person's e-mail message about the connection it said under her details that she did not want to be contacted, but only later did it occur to her how strange it was that she didn't even consider checking her account settings on the company's website. Befuddled, she thought, nearly overwhelmed by the potential consequences of having started this process at all.

I'm sure I'm right and the ball is in my court, she thought, so I'm not at the mercy of somebody else. But hot on the heels of this thought came the realisation that whatever her settings, if her connections were told her name there was nothing to prevent someone looking her up on the Internet and finding her. And what would she do if that half-brother sent her a message from Facebook, perhaps, and asked if she wanted to meet for a coffee? She tried to imagine finding that private message when she logged on to Facebook and how she would react. Would she do it? And what about Frank Wilson, who was obviously her biological father, would he try to find her? Would the Wilson family discuss her? And what about Mrs Wilson and her reaction, if she were still alive? Even the Wilson siblings' relationship with their father might change, because obviously they would know now their father had had an extra-marital affair. The more she thought about it, the more complications she found. The only thing totally certain was that her dad would always be her dad, and nothing could change her feeling of certainty about that.

I'd never be able to resist if one of them found me somehow, thought Amy with a wry smile half an hour later, after pacing restlessly around the flat. It doesn't matter how risky it would be, and how much she didn't want her dad to find out, the chance of getting acquainted, particularly with her biological parent was irresistible.

She closed the laptop and went to bed, but sleep evaded her. In her mind random thoughts tumbled over each other and presented different viewpoints and new angles, but the thing that stood out most clearly was that nothing must connect her current friends and her dad with this second family. When she finally fell asleep. she dreamt of walking into her office and finding a new client standing beside her desk waiting for her, a woman who introduced herself as Delia Wilson. In her dream she screamed and stumbled backwards out of the door before she turned and ran. She woke panting and wondered why in the dream she had run away, as if Deliah presented a threat. It took a long time to go back to sleep and when she woke in the morning she felt exhausted.

15

The following weekend, after not having seen Ben for a few days, she decided to buy the paper and read his weekend column. She knew he usually wrote it in the last two days of the week because he had told her that what he called his real work, which was the political commentary, took up most of his time, so he usually cobbled together his Ben_son column on the Thursday night or even Friday morning. It wasn't that she was checking the content, she just wanted this little contact with him, like a remote touch of his hand.

What she read made her feel a mixture of anger and loss. He had taken nothing of what she had said on board; he still thought it was all right to make named or easily identified individuals the target of his sarcasm.

· · ·

These mothers, who make money out of often staged videos of their cute little children. And the mother, whether in designer gear or a track suit, portrayed as perfect mother who never has any trouble raising her babies and who never loses her patience. The clips of this artificial version of their lives are sick making and cute at the same time. There are some who are genuine, of course, but the ones with the biggest following and who make money from it, are often the famous women, already with an online following. Like a well-known TV host, who had triplets last year. Endless clip of her in active wear (with make-up and false lashes on) bathing and putting her little cherubs to bed. When in reality they have a live-in maid and a live-in nanny, partly thanks to her wealthy husband, and she certainly doesn't put them to bed at night after their bath. She's live on TV five nights a week and usually off somewhere in the weekends to somebody's manor house, definitely not accompanied by the triplets. But she hands out endless advice from her vast fund of experience about how to raise babies and makes money from advertising on her channels. I'm sure she loves them, but they seem to be a business rather than a family.

And then there's active wear. The preferred everyday garb of the kind of woman, who doesn't go to the gym or go for runs but wants people to think she does. Those women just half starve themselves to be super slim and like to appear in the supermarket or in a cafe in skintight active wear and take selfies wherever they go. They're in effect just showing off and taunting those who aren't so slim - and acting out a pretence at the same time.

Because their slim physique isn't due to hard work in the gym, it's due to deliberately under-eating. A good example of this is HL, well-known TV presenter, who often choses this style of dress despite declaring publicly that she wouldn't go near a gym to save her life, thereby not only living a pretence and showing off, but also being dismissive of those who struggle at the gym in order to lose weight. Active wear in public, unless women are out jogging or really going to or coming from the gym, is the shallow, ego-enhancing behaviour of selfie queens, who probably feel they don't exist if they don't share their appearance daily on social media, like HL does on a regular basis.

What upset her wasn't the content or the ridiculing tone of the writing, it was the naming and shaming of a person. Amy agreed with his opinion of why some women wore so-called active wear in public, but the way he once again singled out individuals, who were easily identified though he didn't name them, had a nasty undertone. She wondered if he had a personal issue with HL, maybe she broke up with him or turned him down? It came across like personal revenge, but if that wasn't it, then it was still insensitive and unkind. She felt he had taken nothing she had said onboard, learned nothing and would therefore not change, so a continuing relationship with him would be impossible. However much she had tried to convince herself that this disparity of opinion was something she could put to one side and learn to live with, she had to admit to herself that it was impossible.

Maybe she was too sensitive and didn't understand what others regarded as acceptable, but she thought of the comments when she had lunch with Kate and her friends at the Southbank Centre and decided it might be a gender thing. The men that day had found nothing objectionable in the instances they discussed. But whatever the reason, the gap was too big for her to pretend it didn't matter, far removed from having different opinions about politics or food and she must end this now.

When a text from Ben arrived mid-afternoon asking if she was free for dinner, she didn't reply. A couple of hours later he called, and she didn't take the call, dropped the phone as if it was too hot to hold and went into the bathroom and cried. Why am I crying in the bathroom? she asked herself as she washed her face with cold water. Who am I hiding from? She couldn't face telling him once again what she objected to and that their affair must end. The idea of him trying to persuade her to change her mind, to make light of her concern, was intolerable. She would cry and hesitate and become an object of pity or maybe even revulsion. She simply couldn't face it.

Looking at her blotchy face in the mirror she knew she must sever the connection however hard it was. She had to carry out her campaign even though she knew it would break her heart to lose Ben, but she felt she had no choice. She didn't want to demolish him, but she had to do something. It was easy for Ben to make fun of people from behind his protective armour of anonymity, but it was very hard for his victims to respond in any way apart from on their personal social media. And even if people did that, like she could have done on Facebook or Instagram, others might see it as moaning or not being able to take a joke, and he would never know they had protested. That was the injustice in this situation, his victims' inability to respond or challenge him or even know who he was.

She opened the Word file with draft for her Readers' Comments page comment and fine-tuned it until she was satisfied it struck the right balance, not nasty or punitive but calm and reasoned and with examples. Then she copied and pasted it into the form on the newspaper's website where readers could upload their comments. She had to re-edit it to fit the maximum word limit, but in the end she felt she had done a decent job of it. Giving herself no time to change her mind she pressed the Go arrow, then she picked up her phone and blocked Ben's number.

Two days later, just after she got home from work, and having no idea how many times he might have texted or called, his voice came out of the speaker in the kitchen where people could talk to her from the entry phone downstairs. 'We need to talk, Amy. I want to know why you've blocked me, what I've done. I have thought and thought, and I can't figure it out. Would you please let me in?'

After listening for a few seconds and without replying with a single word she pressed the Off button, but she couldn't move away. She simply stood there leaning her forehead against the wall with tears rolling down her cheeks, as if his voice might suddenly come through the speaker again. The second time this happened, at nine in the evening the next night, when she knew he could see lights on in her flat, she had to force herself to put her finger on the Off button and press it, and it felt as if she was stabbing herself.

When she came home from work the following afternoon there was a large bouquet of beautifully wrapped flowers propped up against her door. She felt sure she knew who they were from and wondered how the messenger had got into the building, but presumably they had some way of delivering to apartment buildings. Instead of unwrapping the flowers completely she just undid the top and stuck her hand in to find the note she knew would be tucked in between the flower stems. "Please tell me what I've done wrong. You've cut me off and I'm devastated. Just leave me a text message if you can't bear to talk to me, but I need to know what caused this. I love you, Ben.

On the way to work the next morning, much later than she usually left in case Ben was waiting outside, Amy made a detour to the florist who had sent the flowers. She walked in with the still wrapped flowers in her hand and the woman behind the counter stared at her with an expression that nearly made Amy laugh, but presumably very few people walk into a florist shop carrying a bunch of flowers.

'These were delivered yesterday,' she said and gave her name and address. 'Can you please tell me if they were ordered online. I mean, do you have the details of the person who bought them. And if you do, I'd like you to notify him that I've returned the flowers and the card.'

'What do you want us to do with the flowers?' The woman's eyes were sparkling with curiosity and mischief. 'Any message?'

'No message, just tell him they were returned. You can take the flowers home if you like, they're perfectly fine and I left them wrapped up overnight - they've been sitting upright in their little pouch of water.'

A few weeks later over lunch at the V&A Kate brought up the Ben_son column again. 'You know how we talked ages ago about that guy Ben_son and his column, remember that? I don't know if you've read it since, but my goodness! Someone's set in motion an avalanche of criticism and comments on the paper's Readers' page, and it's everywhere now. I've even seen posts about it on Instagram. It's like one single reader's comment started a movement. Very interesting to see how these things work.

Having a starting point for the escalation made it a bit like a research project, because I'd never thought of the exact process before – you know, how these things get traction and go viral.'

'No, I haven't seen it - I don't buy the weekend paper.' Amy tried to sound uninterested. 'And nothing's popped up on my social media, so I hadn't heard about it. I'll have a look when I get home.'

They talked about other things and when they were parting to go their separate ways, Kate paused. 'Why don't we walk along to the Natural History Museum, and check out the wildlife garden? Have you seen it?'

'I didn't know there was a wildlife garden.' Amy tried to smile, exhausted after keeping up a cheerful facade over lunch. 'I hope they've got tigers – I love tigers. So much more ferocious looking than lions.'

'It's just wild plants, no tigers - sorry! Or more correctly a huge collection of British plants from all over the country. They started it about twenty years ago, but it's a very soothing place. I haven't been there since early spring.'

Walking walked down Cromwell Road Amy's mind was churning with worry and emotion. She found it impossible to concentrate on what Kate was saying, but she had a strong feeling there was a secondary motive behind the suggestion of going to the wildlife garden. She hoped it had nothing to do with Simon, that he hadn't somehow come across Kate somewhere and been rude and aggressive. That thought had been in the back of her mind ever since the episode in the cafe when he had called Kate a surprising little butterball. He wasn't a man who let a slight remain unanswered, and she really hoped that Kate hadn't been exposed to his venom.

But nothing of that kind surfaced as they started up one of the paths in the wildlife garden, and Kate seemed calm and content. I was imagining things, thought Amy and glanced sideways at Kate, it was just my natural worry about everything just now, the mention of Ben's column, and then thinking of Simon and his dreadful personality.

After a few minutes Kate spoke without looking at Amy. 'What's wrong, Amy? Something's wrong, I could tell last time we met - and it's still the same today. You seem sad.'

Amy had to make a split second decision about whether she should deny being sad and just brush it off as due to pressure at work, or if she should blame her sadness on something other than Ben. She had never mentioned her relationship with Ben to anyone apart from Pete and Roger, just kept it firmly under wraps to avoid questions later in case it didn't last, but on an impulse she decided to be honest, or at least partially honest.

'I *am* sad. I'm sorry I couldn't hide it better - I hope it hasn't ruined our lunch. I fell in love with someone who's impossible. We have no future, and though I love him deeply, I know I have to stay away from him because it would never work – we're too different.'

Kate was silent for a few moments looking

straight ahead, but then she turned and glanced at Amy. 'It's not Simon again, I hope? Surely you aren't still in love with him?'

'Oh God, no! Don't worry about him - that's well and truly over, and don't forget I was the one who broke it off. No, this is a new man, someone I met at a party.'

I'm not going to tell her any details, she thought, but I can give her a bit of an idea. 'I was attracted to him nearly from the very moment I met him, but I knew a few things about him that weren't so good, and I should never have agreed to meet him a couple of weeks later. I should have just stayed clear of him, but I was stupid. We had a short relationship, and I fell into a deep pit of love that I'll probably never be able to climb out of. And then I broke it off – and I think I broke my heart in the process.' Her voice was cracking on a sob, and she stopped talking, unable to face crying in a public place.

'Oh no - how awful for you! It sounds like something you'd read in a novel. So, you just told him it was over?'

'I told him nothing - I just ghosted him. I couldn't bear telling him to his face. I would have cried and made a spectacle of myself, and then he might have tried to persuade me not to break off, and it would have become agonising and painful. I couldn't handle it.'

'What did you do?'

Amy cleared her throat and made an effort not

to sound pathetic. 'I didn't respond to his texts, and then he called, and I didn't take the call. Then I blocked him on my phone, and he came to the flat and pressed the bell by the street door and I just turned the speaker off in the kitchen. I didn't respond with a single word. And then I went into the bathroom and cried and cried.' She hesitated for a moment. 'And sometimes in my sleep I hear his voice – like an echo of the love I had and lost.'

'Let's sit down on this bench for a few minutes.' Kate put her hand briefly on Amy's arm. 'You don't have to tell me any details, let's just sit here quietly and look at the plants and listen to the bees. There's nothing I can do for you apart from just be here in case you want to talk about it, now or at some later date.'

'Thank you!' said Amy on a stifled sob. 'And I really mean it. You're the most amazing friend and you've become so important to me. Maybe sometime in the future, when this doesn't hurt so much, I'll be able to tell you who it was and what it was all about - why it's so impossible. But not now, it's too soon.'

16

Every morning Amy told herself that the feeling of grief and loss would diminish over time, and she would gradually get over what she had done and what she had lost. But rational thought held no sway over her emotions and nothing she told herself was working. A new habit had sprung up out of nowhere, and now whispered conversations with herself took place in the shower and in bed at night and sometimes even while she was sitting in her living room staring blankly at the television without turning it on. She had no idea why these whispered thoughts made her feel slightly comforted, but they did. It was less intrusive and seemed less crazy than talking out loud to herself, but it still imparted a sense of comfort that she so badly needed, like having someone to talk to.

Ben had sent two emails from the company website, where Amy in her role as a senior forensic accountant had an individual e-mail address for direct contact. Both times he asked her to get in touch, said that he just wanted to talk and to try to understand what had happened. In the second message he ended by saying, 'this is the last time I try, or I might turn into a stalker. Don't worry that I will turn up at your street door or at your office. I promise I'd never do that.'

But this morning her despondent routine was interrupted by a text message from Patrick, who had been silent for a couple of weeks while he was out of the country on two jobs in France. 'Are you free for dinner tonight? I have a problem which I'd like to discuss with you.'

Of course I'm free, thought Amy with a wry smile. I've been nothing but free for weeks now. 'I'd love to see you,' she texted back. 'Where and what time?'

When she arrived at Patrick's favourite restaurant that night she sensed immediately that something was troubling him deeply. She gave him a hug and said nothing until they were seated, when it became clear that he didn't know how to start telling her whatever was on his mind.

'Something's happened,' said Amy and reached over the table to grip his hand. 'What's wrong, Patrick? I can tell it's something serious.'

'Oh God, I don't know where to start. My sister sent me a link to a gossip column from a tabloid she sometimes buys - heaven knows why. It seems to be a disgusting mix of gossip and scandal, but it turns out that they occasionally publish photos of me - and of you.'

'Of me? Oh, I see, you mean photos of me with you. But what's the problem? Isn't that why we meet in these well-known places?'

Frown creases appeared between Patrick's perfect eyebrows. 'Normally yes, but this is a bit different, and my sister told me it's not the first time they have hinted that there are rumours I'm a closet gay. This time the headline was "Is he or isn't he?" And under the picture of us they had a line which went something like this, "is she gorgeous camouflage or a genuine lover?" And I thought I should tell you, just so you know it's being said, by some.'

'I don't mind in the least,' said Amy, because though it was obviously distressing Patrick, it didn't reflect badly on her from whatever angle you looked at it. 'Why did you think I would mind?'

'Well, if it blows up and goes viral it could become irritating and it would make you more visible so to speak, so you might get asked about it. Asked to comment, I mean.'

'I don't mind at all. Tell me what you want me to say if I *do* get asked about it, I'll say whatever you want. This is about you, not about me.' She tried to inject some humour into the conversation and added with a little smile, 'I could say that I never discuss my sex life, which might make them draw conclusions without me telling any lies.'

But she could tell that Patrick was not comforted by this. The worried creases remained between his eyebrows, and he looked down for a moment as if he was trying to decide what to say next. When he finally looked up he gazed steadily into her eyes.

'This might seem mad to you, but the agency guys are seriously worried. They know people don't care if someone's gay or not, and I don't particularly mind myself if people wrongly think I'm gay, but they think I'll get far fewer jobs unless this rumour dies down quickly. Not because of the gay aspect - because of the closet aspect. It's unacceptable these days and they're sure the effect would be damaging.'

'Aha - now I get it. I couldn't understand why being gay would matter, but I can see that concealing it would be seen as very off-trend if there's such a word. Like being deceitful or cheating.'

'Exactly, that's it in a nutshell.'

When a waiter appeared just then they quickly scanned the menu and placed their orders. Amy felt helpless and could think of nothing constructive to say. Presumably, if the agency felt so strongly about it and Patrick seemed so genuinely worried then the issue was a real threat, but she couldn't think of anything useful she could do. They talked about other things and even managed to laugh a couple of times at the stories Patrick told her about his jobs in

France, and when they left, earlier then they would normally, she impulsively put her hand on his arm and turned him towards her. She wrapped her arms around his neck right there, just outside the door where everyone inside would see them and kissed him passionately. His first reaction was to stiffen in surprise, but then he entered into the kiss, put his arms around her with one hand on the back of the head, and she felt his nearly silent chuckle while they kissed. After a minute she tilted her head back and looked up at him with a smile full of mischief. 'Again?' He didn't answer, he just took her face between his hands and then his lips were back on hers.

When they finally walked away hand in hand, she said, 'Sorry if that wasn't part of your plan, but I couldn't resist the opportunity while we were still in the bright light at the door. And you're a great kisser Patrick, even if you don't want to do anything else but just kiss.'

'It was lovely!' He squeezed her hand. 'You're a great kisser, too. I do enjoy physical contact, though probably not in the way others do when they get all revved up and feel sexy. I hope someone inside had a phone in their hand and got a shot of us.'

She giggled. 'Probably guaranteed, I'd think – that's why I did it.'

When they parted at the tube station Amy had a sudden idea pop into her head and without considering it in any detail she said, 'Hey, listen! I know someone who might have some idea about how to deal with this problem of yours. My friend Kate – she's about my age, perhaps a year or two older, and she's got this unusual way of looking at things. She sorted out a problem for me once in a most unexpected way, and she's given me some very good advice. I'd like to introduce you to her if you don't mind, and if you like her and trust her you might tell her about this. I won't tell her, that's not for me to do, but maybe you could explain it to her and see what she says.'

'I'll think about it,' said Patrick when they parted, but Amy really didn't expect that he would agree to meet Kate. Such a crazy thing to suggest, she thought as she waited for her train - to ask him to meet a woman he's never met and tell her his innermost problems. He must have thought I was mad! Meeting a stranger and confiding in her without anything more than my recommendation, no, he'll never do that, God knows why I suggested it.

The next morning a text message from Patrick arrived while she was getting dressed. 'I'd like to meet your friend Kate. If you trust her, so do I. I'll take you both out for dinner somewhere quiet where we can talk. And BTW, this might be the bravest thing I've ever done.'

Text message from Melissa: *I see you're dating Patrick despite the vanity ...* This was followed by a smile emoji and a heart.

Amy replied: *We're very good friends, he's a lovely guy.*

Two days later Amy, Patrick and Kate sat at a round table in a small Italian restaurant a few blocks from Amy's flat, a place she had chosen because it was tiny and usually quiet. The evening turned out to be unexpectedly entertaining with Kate and Patrick clearly enjoying each other's company and already teasing each other mercilessly.

At half past ten they were the last people there and seeing how well the other two were getting on, Amy suggested they go back to her flat for a nightcap or another cup of coffee. Walking abreast on the empty sidewalk through the blustery evening the conversation between the other two continued. Amy listened to Kate and Patrick exchanging opposing views on the political situation in a relaxed and friendly way rather than debating it. They're quite alike she thought, they're both kind and thoughtful. This might turn into a friendship. I do hope he decides to ask her advice at some stage in the future.

While she made coffee in the kitchen she picked up snatches of their conversation, but no detail, just the occasional word. She carried a tray into the living room just in time to hear Patrick say, 'So the stumbling block is the *closet* thing – that's what it all hangs on. That's what my agent's really worried about, because it'll make me seem like a fraud. As if

I'm not honest about being gay, even though I'm not gay. And I don't know how to get past that. I'm not totally comfortable telling the whole world that I am what's loosely called asexual.'

Amy quietly put the tray on the table and went back to the kitchen for a plate and some of the almond shortbread biscuits she had bought a few days ago. Leaving the two of them alone seemed like a good idea, so she took her time. When she entered the living room for the second time, they were both laughing. Kate caught her questioning look and said coolly, 'I've just suggested to Patrick that perhaps he should get married. He's told me about his problem - I mean his physical anomaly - so a marriage of convenience might work well.'

'I think she's right, but the problem is finding someone who's willing to marry me and carry out this charade, someone I like enough to live with – and who doesn't expect sex.'

'Are you living on your own or sharing an apartment?' asked Kate with a head tilted to one side the way she often did when she asked a question. It made Amy smile because Kate with her head to one side like that looked very much like a chubby sparrow.

'No, I live on my own. I've earned plenty of money over the last few years and I bought a lovely two bedroom apartment a couple of years ago. Reasonably central and very expensive, but I've never had anybody share it with me.'

Amy didn't know if she should get involved in

the conversation at this stage, because it was quite possible that Kate would come up with other suggestions, and she didn't want to interrupt the flow. She put their coffee mugs in front of them with the biscuits in the centre of the table and sat down in the second armchair from where she could see them both. Patrick was leaning back in the sofa with his long legs stretched out under the coffee table and Kate perched, again a bit like a sparrow, on an armchair that was slightly too high for her.

And at the very moment when Amy thought how uncomfortable she looked, Patrick suddenly said, 'For God's sake, Kate - why on earth are you sitting in that chair? It's far too big for you. Come and sit on this squishy sofa, so at least your feet reach the floor.'

Kate laughed and slid off the chair. 'You're absolutely right. I knew the moment I sat down that I'd made a bad choice, but then I had this thought that if I moved to the sofa, which I can see is far more suitable, you might think I was making advances.'

They looked at each other and burst out laughing again. Patrick reached out and put his hand on Kate's arm and said quite casually, 'Would you like to be my convenience bride? I know this is sudden and you don't have to answer, regarded as a joke, if you like. You can have a huge bedroom with a walk-in wardrobe and a fabulous bathroom all to yourself - or I can come and live in your spare room.' And then he blushed and said quickly, 'Good

Lord, pay no attention to all that rubbish please! I think I must have had to drink too many.'

An hour later after more laughter and chatting about non-traumatic things, Kate and Patrick left to share a taxi and Amy went to bed and, for once, straight to sleep.

Two days later another email from Ben arrived at work: 'I see you're in a new relationship. Over and out. Ben' And once again she heard his voice in her head, that distant echo of love.

17

Every now and again Amy would spend a weekend at her father's flat above the antique shop, sleep in her old room where she spent her entire childhood from the age of three, when her mother died. She had no memory of the move from the bigger flat to the shop, so all her memories of growing up were connected to this little flat with two bedrooms and a combined kitchen and living room.

She would come back from school walk through the shop, talk to her dad and go upstairs to have a drink of milk and help herself to a biscuit before she did her homework. Sometimes she did her homework sitting behind the counter in the shop, and over the years she had learned a lot about antique silver and furniture as if by osmosis. By the time she was sixteen she often helped in the shop in the school holidays when her father went to auctions and garage sales. The elderly friend, who took care of the business when her dad was absent for more than a day died when Amy was seventeen and after that she would take a day off school rather than have the shop closed on a weekday.

This cold, late September weekend Amy had come to look after the shop, so her father could stay upstairs and get over his cold without sneezing over everything. She had arrived the previous evening and been shocked to see how unwell he looked. Thinking back, she couldn't remember ever seeing him look really ill before, not like this. Now, as she studied her father's face she wondered if she should have this discussion with him. She had thought about it for a couple of weeks, and she really wanted to discuss it with him, but it was hard to predict how he would react when he heard what she had done. In the back of her mind sat a hard little lump of guilt that hadn't dissolved over time. She admitted to herself that to some degree she had acted from a desire to punish Ben for what he had written about her, but in the main it was a genuine wish to try to change him, though explaining the difference to her father might not be easy. It was hard to sort out her motivations even to herself and telling him so it made sense might be impossible.

Her father was eating toast with one hand and holding the weekend paper with the other, and Amy knew he would be reading the financial page, totally concentrated and unaware of her scrutiny.

'Dad, listen,' said Amy, having finally made the decision to broach the subject. 'I've got something I want to talk to you about.'

'Yes? Right now?' From the way he looked at her she could tell that he was trying to assess how urgent this was, and if he could delay it until he had finished whatever he was reading. For once Amy decided that her needs must come first.

'Yes, right now. It's kind of embarrassing and you might feel disappointed in me, but I really do need to talk to you about it. And if I don't do it now, I might chicken out and never tell you.'

'Good heavens,' said her dad and put the paper down on the chair beside him. 'Have you done something silly?'

'I don't know if you'd call it silly - it's a long story, so maybe we'll make another cup of coffee and go and sit by the fire. I don't have to open the shop for another hour and a half which gives me lots of time to tell you. I think I've been unnecessarily nasty to someone, and I'm not quite sure how I should deal with it.'

While Amy tidied up and made fresh coffee, her father lit the gas fire at the living room end, something he rarely did in the daytime even in winter when he was more likely to rely on the central heating.

'This is more comfortable,' he said when Amy brought their fresh cups of coffee. 'I can see you've got something difficult to tell me.'

They sat down in the old leather chairs by the fireplace, but Amy found it difficult to start. After a silent couple of minutes, while she looked absently at the flames, she said, 'I don't know if you're aware of a column in one of the weekend papers called Ben_son's Column.'

'Never heard of it - you'll have to explain what this Benson writes about. Is it one of those columns that appear every week?'

'Yes. It's in the weekend edition, every week, but you probably don't read it – not your kind of thing. This guy writes very funny and sarcastic observations about life and people and ... things. And he wrote a paragraph or two about me.'

Her father sat up straight and leaned forward, instantly curious. 'He wrote about *you*? What did he write - and why?'

'Well, there's a back story to this, so hold on.' Amy wished that she had started further back, it would have made more sense. 'The thing is that I've written four romantic novels. The first two were only published as ebooks online, but they generated a bit of a following, so I started offering them as paperbacks as well via an online company that supplies libraries and book shops.'

'Are they doing well?' Now his face was alive with interest, and she could tell he expected a positive story, not something as potentially upsetting as he had first feared.

'They *are* doing well. I sell a lot of ebooks and the paperbacks a selling slowly but steadily too. So now there are four books out there, and they're all under my pen name, which is Julia Somerset.'

'Ah, your mum's maiden name. That's nice.'

She drank some coffee to give herself time to think of how to launch into the next part. 'Anyway, that's what started all this. This Benson guy, and by the way that's not his real name, wrote about Julia Somerset, holding her up as an example of totally ridiculous literature for birdbrains. The kind of stories that would never happen in real life, too romantic and with endings that are too perfect. And he ridiculed the formulaic plots with misunderstandings between lovers, who then sort it out and then eventually comes a happy ending after some steamy sex - or my case not very steamy sex, more by implication than description. What he wrote was supposed to be funny, but it was a very hurtful thing to write about a named person.'

'But why did he pick on you?'

'I don't think he did, he just read one of those romance ebooks at random. He wanted to write about romance writers for some reason, and he just grabbed one of mine on some online platform and ridiculed the writing and the content. After some feedback from his readers, he then quoted passages out of the book on the comments section of the online edition of the newspaper, to prove how ridiculous the book was. Looking back on it now, I can see that the original column wasn't bad as a sarcastic analysis of the genre.'

'But if you write under a pen name nobody

would know it was you, who wrote that book he made fun of, would they. Or do your friends know that it's your book? Is that what's upset you?'

'Nobody knows I'm Julia Somerset, literally nobody. I was upset on my own behalf of course, but also from the point of view of all the other areas of life where he's poked fun at people, made them seem silly and probably made them feel ridiculous - or even devastated. So, when I met him over lunch at a friend's place I decided to teach him a lesson.'

'In public? You had a go at him over a lunch table?' Her father looked horrified.

'Oh God no, I'm far more devious than that, dad – give me some credit for being subtle! I could see he fancied me, so I played along with it, and we had a brief but quite enjoyable affair over the next two or three months.'

Amy had decided to describe her affair with Ben as casual and not very meaningful on the train to her dad's place. The idea of confessing how deeply hurt she was on an emotional level was unthinkable, pity or sympathy had to be avoided. 'Then I wrote a piece for the same paper where he publishes his blog, for the page online where they publish opinions from readers,' she continued.' I wrote a pretty scathing analysis of a heartless man, who makes fun of others and ridicules their efforts and thinks he's clever without a thought for how it affects those he writes about. At the same time, I ghosted him, blocked him on my phone and decided to have nothing more to do with him.'

Her father was silent, clearly considering what she has told him, but after a moment his focus was back on her. 'What name did you put under that opinion you wrote?'

'I signed it "anonymous" because I wanted to see how it would be picked up. They let you do that provided you give them your real name when you submit your comment. I didn't say I was an author or that Julia Somerset's my pen name, for good reasons. If there were comments I wanted them to be seen as general, not linked to my pen name and what he wrote about me, because it could be seen as just my own hurt feelings. I know it was petty, and I should have simply swallowed the ridicule and pretended it had never happened, because in the greater scheme of things it didn't really matter, but I was so upset about how callous he was. The way he used others and their efforts just to make people laugh. I wanted to punish him as well as demonstrate something. And I *had* already tried several times to make him see how awful it was for the people he mocked, particularly if he named them, but he didn't take it onboard.'

Once again her father silently looked into the fire, and she wondered what was going through his mind. Was he disappointed in her? Did he think she had gone too far, been too revengeful and nasty? But he surprised her, as he often did. 'I think you did the right thing, and you've probably taught him a lesson and made him realise he needs to consider people a bit more when he writes his column. Did anyone else comment on what you wrote?'

'I don't know. I haven't checked, but I've heard that there's been quite a bit of noise about it on that online page they call Reader's Notes, but not exactly what. I simply don't want to read or think about it now. As far as I'm concerned it's over. And there's no way I can tell if he's linked it to me, but I think it's unlikely because he doesn't know that I'm Julia Somerset.' She thought for a moment. 'Or maybe he's found out somehow, but he simply hasn't talked about it. When he realised that I'd blocked him on my phone he sent flowers with a note, a sweet note, but I took the flowers back to the shop they had come from on my way to work the next morning. I wrote "return to sender" on the envelope with the note and asked them to inform him that the flowers had been returned. They said nobody had ever done anything so strange before.'

'Do you think they told him?'

'I think so.' Julia gave him a wry smile. 'I could tell the woman in the shop was very intrigued and wondered what the story was, so I think she probably did tell him. She probably read his note too.'

'And apart from feeling bad about making that move to teach him a lesson, are you missing him?'

As he had many times before, her father had sensed more than she had told him and knew there was more to this story than what she had revealed. To avoid looking straight at him, Amy turned her head slightly to the side as if she was looking out the window. 'I miss him so much it feels as if someone hacked off one of my arms,' she said sadly. 'I wasn't going to tell you that, but now I have anyway. I think he was exactly the right man for me, except for that inability to understand how much he hurts people sometimes. And now I've lost him.'

Shivering on the platform at the end of the day in the damp autumn wind, Julia caught a brief glimpse of a tall, sturdy man and her heart leapt in her chest, but of course it wasn't Ben. She kept thinking she saw him, but it was just someone with the same build in a crowd or on the other side of the street. Every time her heart did a little flick inside her, and she remembered how much she had loved being held against that solid chest. The way his hands on her back would hold her to him and make her feel that nothing bad could happened to her. Sometimes she woke in the middle of the night and wondered if she would ever feel so safe and loved again, if there would ever be another man like him in her life. But Ben would move on, he thought she had ghosted him because she had fallen in love with someone else, and he would never find out why she had cut him out of her life so suddenly.

Telling her father the whole story had made her realise that her feelings for Ben, what she had done and the loss she now felt, was such a complex mix and so muddled that she might never be able to deal with it. Back at the flat she closed the door, dropped her bag on the hall floor and burst into tears. Move on girl, she told herself after a few minutes and blew her nose. Put it behind you and stop dwelling on it, this is doing you no good at all. But would she be able to?

18

Only a few days after Amy's visit to her father there was an email alert on her phone just as she was about to leave for work. Standing in the hall with her coat on she fished the phone out of a bag hoping it wasn't from her father to tell her he was ill again. Not that she thought that he would email her to tell her that, but since she saw how ill he looked when she visited she had felt slightly worried about him living on his own. She knew he would laugh at her for worrying and point out that he was only sixty-three and that she lived on her own too.

But the email was from Frank Wilson, the other father, the biological one. As soon as she saw his name she felt a bit panicky and stood indecisively staring at the phone in her hand, unsure of what to do next. If she opened it and read it now, it might ruin her day, make her feel stressed and worried and unable to concentrate. After a few seconds of indecision, she closed the email app, pushed the phone into her bag and set out for work.

But curiosity overcame her apprehension, and as soon as she had hung up her wet coat she closed the door to her office, she sat down at her desk and got her phone out again knowing she would never be able to concentrate until she had read it. The message started simply with her name, no terms of endearment and no formality.

"Amy, I am not sure how you will feel about me contacting you. The discovery that you are my daughter has come as a bolt of lightning from a clear sky. I had no idea your mother was pregnant when she broke off our relationship and left the company we worked at. It has probably taken you completely by surprise too, as I doubt your mother told you about me. I know she died young – someone at the office had heard and mentioned it at work, but not that she had a child. If you would rather not reply, just leave this message unanswered. I will completely understand, and I will make no further attempts to contact you. Should you wish to meet me just one time, or more than once, please tell me when and where. Yours sincerely, Frank Wilson."

Now that Amy had read the message and understood that he was happy to leave the ball in her court and had no expectations, she was relieved and intrigued in equal measure. She decided to let it sit in the back of her mind for the rest of the day and make a decision that evening or maybe the next day to give herself time to think of all the possible consequences of meeting Frank, or whether she should even reply to his message. It was a relief that he seemed so calm and considerate with no display of emotion and no assumption of having the right to meet her. She got up to open her door again only to come face to face with George, who had his phone in his raised hand and a sly smile on his freckled face.

'You're getting famous,' he said, and the smile broadened into open amusement. 'Now your picture is on Instagram as well as on Facebook.'

He turned his phone around to face her and she took it from him. There she was, passionately kissing Patrick in the doorway to the restaurant and whoever posted it had inserted a little trail of red hearts above their heads. The text read: "Has heart-throb model and persistent single, Patrick Lightfoot, finally met his match?" The hashtags that followed were slightly ridiculous and over-the-top romantic.

Amy handed the phone back and grinned back at George. 'We're just good friends,' she said. 'Nothing to get excited about.'

'Yeah, right. *Very* good friends apparently.' George gave her a sly grin and turned to walk back to the reception area, and even from behind she could tell that he was laughing.

Later in the day Stefan winked at her when she looked up as he passed her door on his way to the lunchroom, but thankfully he made no comment. Clearly George had spread the news throughout the office. It was amazing to find that she hadn't given a thought to the consequences when she launched into that smouldering kiss, no restraining instinct to consider how it would affect herself. Very different from how she usually acted, thinking through consequences and potential negative outcomes before she made decisions. But all she had been intent on doing was to create a counter-story to the ones circulating about Patrick and the speculation about his possible in-the-closet status. And, of course, this was what Ben had seen and what had prompted his final message. She cringed at the thought that he now believed she had just cut him off without a word when she fell in love with another man. There was no way she could tell him otherwise, so she would have to live with the knowledge that he despised her and thought she was shallow and rude. Talk about adding insult to injury, she thought, or should it be the other way around? Thinking about it made her feel sick.

After dinner that night Amy finally made a decision, dragged her thoughts away from Ben and replied to Frank's email. "I would like us to meet at least once. Can we meet at the Waterside Café on the Regent's canal on Saturday morning, or in the afternoon if it suits you better? Amy."

She read it through a couple of times and decided it was brief and concise much like Frank's message had been, added her mobile number and pressed Send.

19

In the days since Amy replied to Frank's message she vacillated between wanting to cancel the date and looking forward to it in a slightly remote way. Somehow the whole situation felt unreal, as if it was something she had read about or seen in a movie. She wondered how it would feel and how she would react when she met him in person. Would he want to hug her? Should she pre-empt any attempt at physical contact of that kind by holding her hand out before he did anything, simply start their meeting with a handshake? Somehow even these disjoined speculations seemed purely theoretical, and she couldn't picture the scene in her mind. After a while it occurred to her that the problem was that she didn't know what he looked like, so she googled his name with the word lawyer attached and after sifting through many she finally found him with a Facebook link.

Frank Wilson was tall and slightly stooped with a shock of white hair rising like a cockatoo crest and thick white eyebrows. There were no privacy settings in place on his Facebook page, which surprised her. She scrolled through posts from the last year, only twenty or so and mostly showing Frank with other people, with pictures he had been tagged in. She opened an album of eight pictures that someone called Kirsten Wilson had tagged him in. It appeared to be photos from someone's birthday party with people sitting around a dinner table in a private house and standing, lined up in order of height, in front of a large brick fireplace. Going back and forth between these pictures Amy came to the conclusion that Kirsten Wilson was the daughter of Jonathon Wilson, her half-brother and this was Kirsten's birthday, probably her fifteenth or sixteenth. Jonathon had faded red hair, rising in a crest from his forehead just like his father's, and Kirsten herself had dark red hair, thick and curling on her shoulders just like Amy's. Out of nowhere tears appeared in Amy's eyes and slowly overflowed as she stared at the photo of Kirsten blowing out the candles on a cake. A niece! Well, a half-niece, who looked just like Amy had nearly twenty years ago. She wiped the tears from her cheeks with her fingers and wondered why that girl had affected her so deeply, but it was probably the incredible likeness to herself that had triggered emotion. She copied the photo and saved it on her phone so she could look at it later when she felt calmer.

. . .

On Saturday morning Amy thought she might walk all the way along the Regent's Canal to Regent's Park, but this weather was changeable and what if it rained? Arriving dishevelled and damp to meet her biological father for the first time was unthinkable. Not that it mattered what he thought of her, but she turned her ponderings into a story in her head and imagined Frank telling his children about her, describing her as eccentric to walk a long distance in rain and not caring about first impressions. Stop it! she told herself and nearly laughed out loud. You're not writing a novel now and it doesn't matter if you arrive wet and bedraggled.

When Amy arrived at the Waterside Café, where she had been a couple of times in the past, she recognised Frank right away. He was standing at the windows that look out over the water, an austere figure dressed in dark grey and black, contrasting sharply with the bright light outside and the gaudy floral wallpaper beside the window. Amy stood watching him for a moment and mentally prepared herself, rehearsed her greeting and the handshake, before she approached.

'Frank, hi!' she said when she was a metre or two away and he turned quickly. 'Amy, good morning!' They shook hands and she noted how brittle his bones seemed, as if they were thinner and more fragile than those of other people.

'Let's order and sit down, I'm not having a good

day.' He said it calmly and she realised he was ill. It explained the taut skin on his face, as if there was no layer between skin and skull, and how pale he was. He looked exhausted.

'Why don't you tell me what you want and sit down,' she said. 'I'll go and order. You look tired.'

They spent an hour over tea and muffins, in a conversation with long pauses. Gradually Amy began to understand that Frank felt guilty, as if the affair with her mother had been a one-sided decision on his part. She stopped him when he was halfway through a stumbling explanation of how it had started and impulsively put her hand on his.

'Don't,' she said quietly. '*Please* don't punish yourself. It takes two to tango as my grandmother used to say.' She fished in her bag on the chair beside her while still keeping her hand on his. 'Read this. It's a letter my mother wrote before she died, when I was three. She left it with her sister to give to me when I turned thirty – it got to me a little late, but no matter. Just read it and you'll understand it wasn't a one-sided thing.'

When he handed the letter back she could see how relieved he was. He cleared his throat and drank some of his tea before he spoke. 'I've only told my son Jonathon about you, but for certain reasons I thought he should know. The other two might be upset, but I knew Jonathon would pass no harsh judgements.'

Amy thought she could guess why Frank had

told him and got her phone out of her jacket pocket, found the image she had copied from Facebook and pushed the phone across the table. 'Is this why you told him?'

Frank smiled. 'Of course – and you've done your research, I see. Very smart! I found you online as well and I couldn't believe the likeness between Kirsten and you. I don't know if he'll contact you, but he might if he feels Kirsten should know – he'd obviously make sure you don't mind.'

A few minutes later, in the middle of a conversation about Amy's career, he paused and closed his eyes. Amy watched him visibly pull himself together, realised he was exhausted and was just about to suggest that he might want to go home and rest, when he said, 'I must get home. I'm sorry! I would like to hear more about your life, but my strength isn't what it used to be.'

They walked together to the nearest street and Amy waited with him until a passing cab stopped when she waved it down. 'Look after yourself! I'm glad we met.'

'So am I – a relief from many points of view.' He folded his lanky height into the cab with some difficulty and she closed the door and waited until the car moved away. Rather than take a bus back to the flat she turned and went back into the park, passed the Waterside Café and followed the canal as it wound its way through the park and out the other side. A long walk home, but she needed time to think about all she had learnt during this lowkey and unemotional meeting. Thank goodness his wife is dead, she thought and sidestepped a run-away two-year old pursued by an older sibling. At least he didn't have to explain to her, it must have been hard enough to tell his son when Amy popped up in their email alerts from the DNA company. His children were young when he had the affair with her mother, Jonathon probably ten or eleven, and Delia just a little girl of six or so. And to find that Frank had never known that Amy's mother was pregnant when she left her job at the law firm! There had been no mention in her mother's letter that she never told Frank she was pregnant. She was clever, thought Amy, just what I would have done, create a total separation between the affair and her own life, with no regret apart from the regret of having given in to temptation and had the affair in the first place.

If Jonathon did contact her, she would agree to meet him, as she had with Frank, with no expectation of further involvement, but she had to admit that she would like to meet his daughter Kirsten.

The sun disappeared behind clouds before she was halfway home and she ran through a sudden rain squall to the nearest tube station, strangely calm and relieved after the rather fraught week of worry and indecision.

It was only that evening when she curled up on the sofa to watch a film on Netflix that it occurred to her that in a way her mother had done to Frank what she herself had done to Ben. Cut him off without a word of explanation, though for a very different reason.

20

As the days passed Amy felt as if her emotional life was happening in two layers, separate and different but concurrent. Grief and guilt about Ben in one layer, and in the other relief about how minimal and unemotional her meeting with Frank had been, and how final it had seemed. Her mood swung between these two states of mind, but more than once she caught Stefan's eyes on her with a slightly worried expression however upbeat she tried to appear at work. Being like this had made her realise that she had nearly always been happy and even-tempered before the Ben affair, and now Stefan found her mood hard to understand, when everyone around her assumed she was in a new and exciting relationship after the media interest in her and Patrick.

She had been out with Patrick only once since that kiss in the restaurant doorway, but he texted her now and then to tell her what he was doing. The one time they did get together she asked him if the kiss post on Instagram had taken some of the pressure off him and he laughed. 'It certainly did! A lot of media notice, most of it commenting on you rather than me. Then I went out with another woman twice in the last couple of weeks and people instantly started wondering if I had two on the go at the same time. My agent's very pleased.' They both laughed and Amy was happy for him and relieved he hadn't noticed her strange underlying mood.

But tonight, her mood was low. A howling wind was stripping the last yellow leaves from the trees along the canal, and dusk was rapidly turning to full evening darkness. Leaning her forehead against the kitchen window Amy looked out at the depressing vista and felt as if the weather and the season had been perfectly designed to match her mood. The whole week had been a struggle and the need to keep up a good front at work had nearly defeated her. Every smile or light-hearted comment had been an effort, and she had developed a trick of not looking in the mirror while she washed her hands in the restroom, because she knew how close tears were, and crying at work was inconceivable. That morning, she had wondered if bathrooms and tears had now become permanently linked in her brain and what she could do to break the link. Maybe lie in the bath and watch a YouTube comedy on my phone, she thought, and then dismissed the idea as nonsense.

Truth and lies, she thought now and turned

from looking out to lean back against the windowsill, gazing vacantly across the nearly dark kitchen. Lately she had felt that dark rooms made her feel calmer, so she avoided turning the lights on until she absolutely had to and then only the lamps on the side tables in the living room and the rangehood light in the kitchen, never the ceiling fittings which would make the place too bright, painfully bright. Truth and lies, she whispered to herself, that's what it is. I lied by omission and didn't tell Ben that I'm Julia Somerset. I carried out my revenge to shine the light of truth on his writing, to show him how hurtful he was. Then I ghosted him and now he obviously thinks it was because I fell in love with Patrick, and I can't tell him that truth either. He will always regard me as shallow and cruel, and I can't do anything about it. Will I feel like this for the rest of my life?

As their relationship progressed her initial idea to re-educate Ben had morphed into a strong desire to simply show him he needed to change, and she had tried several times, but it hadn't worked. Her post on the Readers' Comments web page had been a last resort, the last thing open to her to try to make him see her point of view, to simply make him understand how damaging his sarcastic humour could be. But now she could see that what she had written in that post had resulted in something that was close to taking him down, a phrase that in her mind meant "destroy". She hadn't been able to make herself follow up and read what resulted, but from Kate's comment it sounded as if the debate had gone wide and turned harsh.

How she wished she had decided to tell him to his face that Julia Somerset was herself! Then she could have been forceful and more honest. She could have told him how she had reacted to what he wrote about the romance writer. But it was too late now, she had done what she did, and she couldn't change it, and even if Ben understood what she had been trying to tell him, she had lost him. The way she had gone about it would have extinguished any affection from his side. I did this to myself, she repeatedly reminded herself, I could have done it another way and I chose not to.

Later that evening after half-heartedly preparing a light meal and then only eating half of it, Amy sat in front of the television repeatedly clicking the remote and finding nothing that tempted her. Documentaries were too serious, comedies didn't resonate with her mood, and she couldn't find a film or a drama series that didn't seem either too happy or depressing enough to potentially lower her mood even further.

When her phone buzzed she nearly didn't pick it up. A cheerful conversation with a friend would be beyond her, but when she saw it was Pete calling she put a finger the green circle and said, 'Hi, Pete –

how are you?' and tried to make her voice sound normal, if not cheerful.

'Hi babe,' said Pete and Amy heard Roger in the background saying something that sounded like "sexy beast". 'Would you like to join us at Baluga tomorrow night? That's Baluga with an "a", not Beluga, the middle-eastern place. Susanna Goldman is doing just one night there, and Roger and I have booked a table for six. We've got one other couple, but I thought you might like to come and bring somebody perhaps?'

Susanna Goldman had risen to jazz vocalist fame when Pete and Amy had just started university and got to know each other. She had sung in the student cafe a couple of times, but Amy had not heard her live for several years. This seemed like the perfect antidote to her low mood; an evening with Pete and Roger and listening to Susanna would divert her thoughts. Without hesitation Amy said, 'Yes, please! I'd love to. I've been sitting around at home far too much lately. What time should we meet? And do they serve bar food or just nuts and things?'

'We're planning to have meal there – definitely! They don't have a lot of choice, but their bowl potato wedges with crunchy bacon bits is enough for an OK supper, and they have an ice cream vending machine in the foyer now, so you can even have dessert. And Roger wants to know if you'll bring the sexy beast from that photo on Insta.'

'No, I'm not going out with him now, and he's

already moved on. I'll come on my own.' Appearing in public with two gay guys and Patrick might be tempting fate as far as Patrick's reputation was concerned and cause renewed confusion.

Baluga was crammed and very noisy when Amy arrived the next evening, but she had no trouble spotting Pete and Roger with a couple she didn't know. Right at the front, of course! She grinned as she slowly made her way towards them between the tables, careful to keep her coat close around her.

'I knew you'd be right next to the stage,' she said and sat down on an empty chair between Roger and the unknown woman. 'I'm Amy, hi! Pete always did this at university where Susanna started out at the time we were students – he was right at her feet, always.'

'You two haven't met, have you? Amy, this is Cilla and her husband Ossie the Aussie.'

Amy wasn't sure she had heard right, so leaned over and said hi to the man with the red beard on Cilla's far side. 'Is that Ossie as in Oswald or Aussie as from Australia?'

'Both - Oswald for my sins,' said the bearded man. 'After a grandfather. And Aussie with an A for Australian. Double whammy.'

After a surprisingly entertaining evening Amy got home late and found her mood had lifted. Instead of going to bed she turned on her laptop and started writing, lost to the world for two hours and only snapping out of her fictional world when an email notice appeared in the corner of the screen.

Hi, I'm Jonathan Wilson. Frank told me he'd met with you and that you talked about my daughter, Kirsten. He told my family about your meeting and said how amazingly alike you and Kirsten are, and now she would like to meet you, as would I. It would only be us two. Maybe we could have coffee this weekend? It's up to you, of course. Kind regards, Jonathan.

This needed no thought. Meeting someone who was of the same blood and looked exactly like she had at fifteen or sixteen; how could she resist? She replied and suggested the Gamble room at the V&A because perhaps Kirsten had never been there and it was such an amazing place, close to her own heart. Jonathan's reply came within minutes, so he was obviously up late too, perhaps working. *Thank you, Amy! I look forward to it. See you on Saturday morning, Jonathan.*

21

On Saturday morning, as Amy walked along her customary track across Hyde Park from the tube station her thoughts were far from the coming meeting with her half-brother and half-niece. She was mentally reliving the times she had crossed the park with Ben: the incident with the adoring dog, the time she asked him if he wanted to go to bed with her, and how it had felt to be physically near him. She found herself slowing down when tears suddenly filled her eyes and forced them back with an effort of will. Determined to dispel gloomy musings on the past, she continued walking at a brisk pace, put a smile on her face and concentrated on looking forward.

They were waiting just outside the entrance and Amy had no trouble identifying Kirsten, whose thick mane of dark red curls flowed over her shoulders, bright and nearly startling in the morning sun. As Amy approached and mentally rehearsed what she might say, Kirsten broke away from her father's side and ran towards her, coming to a halt just an arm's length away.

For a moment they stood there, staring at each other in silence, then Amy reached out and pulled Kirsten into a hug, unplanned but irresistible.

'Look at you!' she exclaimed after a moment and held Kirsten away. 'My God, it's like having a little clone!'

'Isn't it great?' the greyish-green eyes, just like Amy's own, glittered with excitement. 'Granddad showed me a photo of you online, from the website of the company where you work, and I couldn't believe it – it's just crazy! It's like I have a sister!'

By this time Jonathan had caught up with them and stopped to study them with an expression of awe and delight. 'Bloody incredible!' he said and got his phone out. 'I hope you don't mind, but my father will love to see this, something to cheer him up in his hospital bed. Just looking at you two is making people smile – check out that family on the other side of the street. All of them just staring at you.'

'Oh no! Is he in hospital?'

'It's his heart again. He'd only been home for a couple of months and now it's playing up again. He hasn't been well for several years.'

Kirsten kept close by Amy's side as they entered the museum and slowed down with an amazed "Oh, look!' when they crossed the long sculpture gallery.

Amy felt her reactions like little physical touches and realised this girl was very like herself in more than looks. In the doorway to the Gamble room Jonathan paused for a moment and let out a quiet "Wow! They were lucky enough to get a table beside one of the pairs of pillars, Amy's favourite place with the enormous, colourful windows to one side and a high arch above them. Kirsten was silently absorbed in studying the room, moving her focus from one side to the other and then up at the high ceiling. 'Beautiful!' she said and turned her gaze to Amy. 'It's like a magic place full of surprises. That ceiling!'

Inside Amy's head she heard Ben's voice saying the same thing when they first came here together, but she pushed the memory aside and smiled at Kirsten. 'I'm so glad you like it! It's one of my favourite places to have lunch or coffee. I thought you might not have been here before.'

'I've never been here before either,' said Jonathan and reached out to touch the tiled pillar just beside him. 'I must bring Penny – don't you think she'd love it, Kirsten?'

'She would! But she's been here – she told me this morning before she went to work.' Kirsten turned to Amy. 'Mum's a police officer, so she works weekends sometimes. She said she's been to the museum a few years ago to see a fashion exhibition with a friend, but they didn't go into the café, so she'd never heard about the Gamble room.'

Jonathan listened to them talking, gazing from

one to the other and back again, as if he still couldn't quite believe it. When their coffee had been served, he took a sip and said, 'I bet neither of you know this, but sitting here watching you I can see more than the similarity in features and hair colour. You have the some of the same mannerisms, too.'

Kirsten grinned. 'Like talking to much? Or maybe laughing too much?'

For the next hour and a half, they talked easily about their work, about school and hobbies and holidays. There were no embarrassing pauses, which was what Amy had feared most, and surprisingly nobody mentioned the affair between Amy's mother and Frank until they were nearly ready to leave.

'It seems so weird,' said Kirsten suddenly. 'You know, thinking of granddad having an affair when he was younger. It's kind of hard to imagine him young and ... whatever he was. And that he never knew your mum was pregnant with you! I mean, why didn't she tell him? Surely he could have helped her with money or whatever she needed, even if they couldn't marry. Dad says Frank told him she left the place where they worked without telling him.'

Amy realised that neither Kirsten nor her father knew that Amy's mother had also been married at the time and decided they deserved to know how it had happened.

'Let's go for a short walk if you have time,' she said. 'We can go along to the gardens at the Natural

History Museum just along the street and I'll tell you about the letter my mother wrote when I was three – I think it's only fair that you know the whole story.'

An hour later, when they parted with a promise to meet again, Kisten embraced Amy and whispered a quiet "thank you!"

Amy turned at the corner and watched them walk away, with Kirsten looking up at her father and talking excitedly. I feel as if I've acquired a daughter, she thought and smiled to herself. She hadn't felt so upbeat and positive for a long time and knew the memory of that final hug from Kirsten would cheer her up when things felt bleak. Like having a happy place for her to visit, something to make her smile.

22

The day after the wonderful meeting at the V&A museum, Amy met her father for Sunday lunch at Monsoon in Greenwich, a café Amy had never heard about. It seemed like an unlikely location and involved a long journey, but seeing he had suggested a café for nearly the first time after usually leaving it to Amy, she didn't hesitate. Something unexpected, that makes two days in a row with surprises, she thought and put the Monsoon address into the navigation app on her phone. Turnpin Lane turned out to be close to the Old Royal Navy College, and as she turned into the lane she could see one of the spired domes of the college at the far end, above some other buildings in the middle distance. Walking down the narrow, flag-stoned lane she thought was an interesting place this was, full of history and drama, but why were they meeting here?

Her father was already in the cafe, seated at a

table by the window with a cup of tea in front of him. 'I got here early,' he said. 'And I've ordered my lunch – tell them you're with me and they'll serve us at the same time.'

Leaving her phone on the table she went to the counter, placed her order and returned to sit down. And noticed her phone showed the image Jonathan had sent her of her and Kirsten together, which she realised she had saved as a lock screen instead of on her home screen. Her father looked up and said quite calmly, 'A half-sister or a half-niece?'

Stunned and unable to even think for a moment, Amy stared at him, and he smiled faintly. 'When did you find out?' he asked at exactly the same time as Amy said, 'How did you know?'

'You fist,' said her dad. 'Did you do the DNA thing? I know you said you didn't see any point, but this was exactly why I said you should do it.'

Amy realised that this was a story of two parts and decided the index event was the letter her mother had written so long ago.

'Two things, really,' she said slowly. 'The first thing was a letter Aunt Susie unearthed when she moved house. A letter mum wrote just about the time I turned three and gave to Susie to keep until I was thirty. I got it a few years late, but it was about me – mum felt I should know. She said you didn't know, but obviously you did.'

Her father said nothing, just waited, so she carried on. 'And then I did the DNA test, and several people popped up as close connections.'

'When?'

'Very recently. I met with Frank – I don't think of him as my father because you're my dad, so I just think of him as Frank. And I met with him once. He's very ill and probably hasn't long to live. He's emaciated and very tired. And he confirmed what mum said in that letter, that she hadn't told him she was pregnant, so he had no idea. It was a very brief affair, only a couple of months, and then she went to another job, so he never saw her again.'

Surprisingly her father said, 'Can you show me that photo again?'

She unlocked the phone and passed it to him, and he took it out of her hand, eyes already on the photo. 'My God, she like a clone of you, just younger! Must be a niece. How old is she?'

'Sixteen,' said Amy with a slight feeling of unreality at this calm interest. 'How much did you know, and how?'

Just then their meals arrived, so Amy tucked the phone back in her bag and waited. As soon as the waitress had gone her father picked up his knife and fork and Amy protested.

'Please don't start eating right away - I can't wait until after lunch, Dad! Or can you tell me while you eat? I really want to know!'

'Of course I can talk and eat. That's what we always do, isn't it? And don't feel so worried – I can see it written all over your face. I've always known, or nearly always, since you were about a year old.'

'But how?'

He smiled and she could see he was far less worried or upset than she was on his behalf. 'You grew thick dark red hair from the time you were less than a year old, wonderful hair, and one day I had one of those moments, you know what I mean – when something just clicks in your mind. You were sitting on the living room floor with your toys, talking away to yourself and I remembered that lawyer at the place where your mum worked when we first got married. I was away a lot in those days, but I'd joined their weekly drinks on a Friday after work once or twice – and I'd met the guy, he was unmistakeable.' He chuckled. 'Hair you could spot a mile away, a very tall chap but quite a bit older than us, at least ten or twelve years, maybe more. And that image in my head made me remember how surprised I was when Dora left that job – a very sudden decision, but she claimed there was no reason, she was just sick of being expected to work so much overtime.'

'But you didn't ask her? When you had that idea, I mean? You didn't say something like "the only other person I've seen with that colour hair was that guy you used to work with"? Or perhaps you felt it was better to wait.'

Her father shook his head, seemingly unconcerned. 'I thought about it, but what would have been the point? She'd left that job - we were still together and as close and happy as we'd always been. Why upset the apple cart?'

While he had been talking a little film clip had

played out in Amy's head, the way it often did when she contemplated reasons and potential consequences. A little clip of her dad sitting there watching his tiny daughter and quietly working it out, considering if it was worth knowing for sure and deciding it wasn't.

'Amazing!' she said. 'You're incredible, Dad! How many men would have been able to do that? Not many, I wouldn't think.'

"It was just common sense – nothing heroic about it at all. I've always felt you were my child, anyway, and I imagine you still feel we're father and daughter?'

There was the tiniest hint of doubt in his voice now, and Amy reached across the table and curled her fingers around his. 'We *are* father and daughter! We've been the best team I can imagine ever since Mum died - we've done everything together and nothing's changed. I've only met with Frank's son Jonathan, who had also had his DNA tested and who appeared as a close contact. And he brought Kirsten, because Frank had shown them a picture of me he found on the internet – because of the likeness. I had coffee with Jonathan and Kirsten at the V&A museum yesterday. It's not as if I expect to have some kind of constant involvement in their lives or they in mine.' She laughed quietly and added, 'Jonathan's wife is not keen on meeting me for some reason, and his sister Delia finds the idea – this is Kirsten's words – "unnatural". But I bet Kirsten will keep in touch by text or whatever. She is very excited about having a half-aunt and being my clone.'

And then the most important thing, the bit she hadn't told him, occurred to her. 'Oh God, Dad! I should have told you right away, I'm sorry! In that letter Mum said how she realised very quickly that the affair was based on lust, and it only went on for a couple of months. She said she came to her senses and knew she couldn't risk what you and she had together for a short term thrill, so she ended it and resigned.'

It wasn't until she was ready to leave to take a train back to town that Amy thought to ask why her father had suggested such an out-of-the-way place to meet, and he grinned. 'An auction in a fabulous old Queen Anne style house where some old lady who'd lived for over sixty years. Full of really good quality furniture and some rather unusual Georgian silver, including a claret jug in a style I've never seen before.'

'Did you buy anything?'

'A truck load – or very nearly. I've just sent some photos to a client who might be interested in the furniture, so we'll see what happens. I just suggested this place because I like Greenwich, and I thought a change of venue would be nice.'

Walking back down Turnpin Lane Amy suddenly remembered an outing when she was very small, maybe five. 'Remember when you and I came here, and I stood on the meridian at the Observatory on top of the hill and then we ran down that long grass slope and I fell and got a bleeding nose?'

'I've got a picture of you standing on Longitude Zero. I'll take a picture of the photo and email it to you - it's a print in the album. You can show it to Kirsten. There you are with your blazing curls standing on one leg – very cute, and she probably looked exactly the same at that age.'

On the train back, travelling on her own again as her dad was going back to the auction house to check on something, Amy felt more relaxed about life in general and congratulated fate on having had the great idea of showing her dad the photo of Kirsten. Couldn't have worked out better, she thought with relief about not having that secret sitting in the back of her mind every time she thought of her father. And then, out of nowhere, came a scent of cinnamon – Ben! But when she looked around he wasn't there, and she felt deeply disappointed and confused. How could that strong smell swirl around her if he wasn't anywhere nearby? After a few minutes she casually let her eyes scan the carriage and a middle-aged man gave her an inviting smile, which she pretended not to notice. There must be an aspect to the smell signature phenomenon which she hadn't understood, yet another dimension.

She thought back to the incident a few weeks ago when she had smelt overheated cooking oil when she was on the underground platform and nearly panicked at the thought of Simon following her around, even though she had deleted the tracking app from her phone. A similar thing had happened then; she had cautiously looked around and met the eyes of a stranger, who smiled as if he knew her. Without returning the smile Amy had turned forward again and tried to make sense of it. The smell had undoubtedly come from him and the look on his face was unmistakeable. Maybe the oil smell was linked to both personality and intention? And why had she never thought of this before?

23

Amy had been so busy with her own concerns and worries as well as the excitement of meeting Kirsten and Jonathan, not to mention her father's astounding revelation, that she forgot about Charlotte's problem until she called one morning.

'Let's meet for a glass of wine,' she said breezily. 'Preferable soon and at your place. Is that OK with you? Perhaps tonight?'

Amy couldn't help laughing at this abrupt self-invitation. 'That's a pretty comprehensive start to a chat! What you're saying is that you're coming to see me tonight and expect a glass of wine – is that it?'

'Exactly! I've got the most surprising thing to tell you, and Caroline is with Roland tonight and he's dropping her at school tomorrow. I need to discuss some complicated stuff with you, and I'd rather do it over a glass of wine. Will half past six be OK? I'll bring wine and snacks.'

Amy put the phone back on her desk and walked out to the reception area where George was talking to someone on the phone and laughing. She leaned on the counter and tried to imagine who he was talking to. Best bet was a girlfriend, next best bet was a mate, and third, but unlikely, was his mum, who often called him at work to ask why he hadn't called her for a couple of days.

'I've no idea why she calls the company number,' George had said a few weeks ago when he told Amy about his overly protective mother. 'She could call my cell phone, so I'd have the choice not to answer if I'm busy.'

'That's why, of course.' Amy grinned. 'That's why she calls the company number – it gives you no choice, you have to answer.'

'Evil,' said George, frowning. 'I'm twenty-two, for God's sake, not a baby.'

But now Amy caught his eye, so he nodded and finished the call he was on, saying, 'Thank you! No, it's Ok, any time! I love talking to you.'

So, not his mother, thought Amy, but it seemed personal, very relaxed. 'Girlfriend?' she asked. 'Definitely not your mum.'

'It's Sharon, and ...' He saw her blank look and smiled. 'Sharon Aldridge - the woman from the Fraud Office you met with a while back.'

Stunned doesn't cover this, thought Amy,

gobsmacked is the word I'm after. How on earth did this happen?

'You've become friends, have you?' she asked casually while playing a little film clip in her mind of freckly, twenty-two year-old and slightly chubby George and the mid-fortyish, dark-suited and definitely no-nonsense woman from the Fraud Office. 'Is she nice?'

George studied her face for a moment before he replied, and she could nearly read his mind: Should he tell her or brush it off?

'We had a very good chat about films,' he said straight-faced. 'She was early the second time she came, and we talked about vampire films for some reason, and then we moved on the splatter movies and discovered we find the same crazy things funny. You know, the kind of things most people find revolting. She's called a couple of times since, but we usually text.' He took in Amy's expression and added apologetically, 'It's probably against company policy or something, but I don't spend heaps of time talking to her at work. She says it brightens up her day when she's dealing with lots of hard stuff at work.' He thought for a long moment and added, sounding surprised. 'I suppose it *is* a bit odd – but she said just now that she knows nobody else who has the same whacky sense of humour, and she wouldn't dare tell her friends – they'd think she was mad.'

Not that Amy could quite picture this unusual

friendship, but it was sweet and funny. 'That's lovely! Unusual friendships are often the best. One of mine, when I was a pre-teen, was the old lady who ran the newspaper stall by the pub. I used to tell her everything if she wasn't busy when I went to get some milk at the corner, all my secrets and worries. And I don't mind at all – I'm just a bit surprised. But good for you, making friends with someone like her. I found her a bit intimidating myself.'

'God no, that's just a protective front! She very funny. What can I do for you?'

'If you go out at lunchtime, could you please pick up a ham sandwich for me? I was planning to work late, but now I've got to be home at a reasonable time, so I thought I'd skip having a lunch break and work right through.'

Back in her office she knuckled down to a very boring piece of analysis and regretted not handing it over to Grant, ate the ham sandwich and drank the nice cup of coffee George put in front of her and sat at her desk without a break until half past five.

'This is nice!' said Charlotte a couple of hours later and leaned back in the reclining armchair by the window where Amy sometimes slept when she had woken up with nightmares. 'God, this chair is such a treat, I could go to sleep. But – are you ready?'

'Could you get started, please? You've been delaying telling this astounding tale ever since you walked in the door and I'm dying of curiosity now. What's happened?'

Charlotte took a sip of her wine and put the glass on the little table beside her, and Amy knew why. This was what Charlotte nearly always remembered to so when she was holding a drink, because her conversations always involved a lot of wide gestures, and she needed both hands free. 'It's Breannah – remember her? Roland's new woman. I told you she wanted to meet me, so I did. We had a drink after work on Friday night when Caroline was at a friend's place for a sleep-over. And what was even more surprising was that she, Breannah that is, asked if the place she suggested was one that Roland ever used to go to!'

'Curiouser and curiouser,' said Amy. 'It's obviously relating to him in some way, and she didn't want to risk him to see you two together.'

Charlotte frowned. 'Exactly right! She wanted to ask me about him, and I didn't know what to say. It wasn't a situation I'd ever imagined I'd be in. I mean, I know how he was with me and why I wasn't devastated when he left, or after a while, I wasn't. But to discuss it with this new love of his? Wouldn't that be unethical – if you can call it that about something private and non-corporate.'

Amy tried to imagine herself in this situation and found it hard. Her relationship with Simon hadn't involved living together, much less a house and a child, so it wasn't comparable.

'I really don't know,' she said slowly. 'If Simon had a new woman who approached me ... yes, I think I would tell him how he was to me. Because he's toxic and dangerous to any woman's self-respect, but maybe not ... honestly, I don't know.'

Charlotte had another sip of wine and reached for the crisps. 'I told her a little bit, just that he tended to be passive-aggressive, but nothing about the many affairs he had. I mean, she was one of them, so she must know he isn't always faithful.'

'There's something you're not saying.' Amy studied her friend's face and saw immediately that she was right. Charlotte was holding something back, but she didn't reply, so Amy ate some crisps and an olive and tried to wait patiently. After a couple of minutes' thought, Charlotte finally spoke again.

'I've never told anyone about this, but I must or this whole conversation won't make sense, I can see that now. So here it is - he hit me a few times, real punches. When he lost his patience if I argued with him.' Then she added quickly as if she wanted to make excuses for Roland. 'He only caused read damage once, when he gave me a black eye and a split lip.'

This seemed incredible and Amy wondered why Charlotte had never told anyone. It seemed incomprehensible that she had kept something so hurtful and damaging to herself, possibly for years.

Her relationship with Roland had always been rocky, with problems of various kinds, which she *had* talked about, so why had she never mentioned that he actually hit her? Instead of commenting, she said, 'Did Breannah say he hits her?'

'No, but she might have if I'd told her that he hit me, don't you think? I held back, though, and then after we parted I thought maybe I shouldn't have. What if she thinks he might one day? If she's caught some early signs, and now she's trying to find out from me if that's likely? What do you think?'

A reasonable angle popped into Amy's head. 'Did she tell you exactly why she wanted to talk to you? I mean, did she give you any examples of things she worried about?'

'No, I tried to find out what was behind it, but all she would say was that he seemed to be what she called "moody" quite often. Which might mean he gave her the silent treatment to punish her for some transgression, or just that he didn't like her not agreeing with him.' She thought for a moment and added, 'Or it could be that he was on the brink of hitting her and tried to control himself. I think he does that quite often – or did when he was with me, I mean.'

An hour later, over an impromptu dinner of pizza from the freezer and salad, with another glass of wine beside them, Charlotte suddenly interrupted a chat about a new Netflix series she had just started watching. 'I *will* get back to her! I'll text her and say, let's meet for a drink again, or perhaps I'll ask her to come to my place one evening. I don't think I want it on my conscience if she moves in with him and then has to extricate herself if it all goes bad – such a hassle!'

my looked hard at her boss, Stefan, who was leaning against the windowsill in her room, where he had stood for the last ten minutes, immovable. 'I wish I didn't have to go. You know how I hate the cold, and the long term forecast said there might be early snow up there, though it seems incredible. Is there really no way we can take care of this without someone actually being on site?'

She studied Stefan's face and knew the answer would be no. He had worked in this field for two decades longer than she had, and if he felt someone had to be on site then that was how it had to be. And he can't go himself, thought Amy, not with this third wife of his having a baby any moment now. He'll want to be there, he absolutely adores her, so he's out of the question, and Grant and the others aren't experienced enough for something tricky and nearly undercover like this.

After a moment she said, 'Sorry, Stefan,' and

smiled at his concerned face. 'I'm being silly. Of course, I'll go. I'll look up how to build an igloo and the symptoms of hypothermia on the internet, so I'm prepared. Let's get a cup of coffee and sit down on your office and map out the best strategy to deal with this, because you haven't told me all the details yet.'

'Right,' said Stefan a few minutes later, 'this is what happened. The company got into financial trouble – a slow but steady process over the last two years, very unexpected and the two owners are having a major disagreement about how to proceed. One of them, Martin, wants to admit they can't pay their creditors and declare themselves voluntarily bankrupt, go into liquidation owing a very considerable amount. Jordan, the guy who called us, says he's sure they can find a way out, borrow more for example, which is meeting with strong resistance from Martin. Jordan is now very suspicious, because he's beginning to wonder how the cash flow could suddenly have got so bad after they made their best profit ever of over a million two years ago. He says they've been "bleeding money, slowly, but a lot". And you and I know what that means, as does he. He's not very tech savvy and he's prepared to pay with his own money for us to go up there and sneakily take their entire system apart without Martin's knowledge.'

'I would have thought he could simply back up absolutely everything from their hard drive on an external backup device and send it to us. Or send it to us from the cloud, where presumably all their stuff is saved.' Amy still couldn't help trying to think of ways to avoid her having to go all that way and then probably do nothing more than instruct the suspicious man how to use a backup device and give her access to their bank.

Stefan nodded. 'I know, it's a pain in the butt, but he's prepared to pay big money because this could mean the difference between being held up as a deficient company director or being able to prosecute his partner for fraud - *if* he can figure out where money went. He's convinced his partner stole it, well, he says he's totally certain, but if he reports it without proper evidence nothing will happen. He needs enough ammunition to get the guy prosecuted - or scare him into giving the money back instead of hiding it in some Cayman Islands account or perhaps in a Bitcoin.'

'OK, I suppose you got your head around this while I had my week's leave, so can you please forward all the email correspondence you've had with him, so I can put myself in the picture before I get there. I might want to ask this guy a few questions of my own too. I'll get George to book a train ticket and a hotel room. What was the date he suggested?'

'It would be quicker to fly, wouldn't it? And he wants you there on the fifth of next month – three weeks from now. It's when his partner is going to be away for a week.'

'OK, then. But no flying.' Amy shook her head.

'No way, not at this time of the year, when we're likely to have bad weather. Flying in a blue sky is horrid, flying in a blizzard would give me a nervous breakdown.'

'Amy, don't exaggerate - blizzards are very rare and I don't think there's one coming now. I'll go back to my office and forward those emails to you. And remember to take a warm coat and gloves.'

That night Amy had just picked up her phone and turned off the living room lights when a text alert pinged, and she opened a text from Charlotte as she walked back to her bedroom. What she read stopped her in her tracks and she exclaimed, 'What!' before she dialled Charlotte and waited impatiently for her to pick up.

'You had a fun evening with Breannah? Really?' she said disbelievingly. 'How did that happen? And where were you?'

Charlotte giggled. 'I thought that would get your attention. Have you got half an hour right now or do you want to come over for dinner in the weekend?'

'I can't wait,' said Amy, ' which you knew, of course. So tell me, how did this come about and what made it a fun evening?'

'You know how I said I must get back to her? I kind of felt guilty that I hadn't been totally open about Roland and his various ways of punishing me for not pleasing him, so I texted her and said something like , "I think we need to talk some more. Can we meet again soon?" and she replied within seconds, and we met last night – here. She came over after Caroline was in bed and she never wakes up, so no risk of her telling Roland. We had a very frank and interesting chat over a glass of wine or two.'

Amy tried to picture them, the wronged wife and the mistress-now-partner getting on, and thought maybe it sounded reasonable, but having fun? 'And how did that go? And what was it that made it a fun evening?'

Charlotte chuckled. 'Bet you won't believe this – I hardly believe it myself, but we might become best friends, Breannah and me. I told her about Roland's outbursts of fury and that he hit me, and she just nodded, as if she was wondering already if that's how he was behind that charming exterior, and she said it's the reason she hadn't let him move in with her when he left me.'

'And what's she going to do about it? Did she say?'

'Oh yes – she was totally frank, right from the start. She's breaking it off right away. She said she doesn't let lust or love run her life, she keeps reason at the forefront at all times and getting into a relationship with someone like him was out of the question. She said her mum forgave an abusive man over and over, she said it was like a circular reference in Excel – which I don't know anything about, but you probably do. And best of all, you'll never guess - she's joining my book club. We like exactly the same kind of films and books, and we had a great chat about a book it turns out we've both read recently – it's called The Ministry of Time, very different and interesting. She's great fun and I think you'd like her too. We'll get together for dinner some time, but not here.' She laughed. 'I can't let Caroline know we've become friends, or she'll tell Roland, and all hell will break lose if he thinks I've sabotaged his new love life.'

'Amazing! Not what I expected at all. I'm looking forward to meeting her.'

'I'm having drinks with her the week after next probably – she wants me to meet her brothers, they'll both be in town for her birthday. And then it's book club the week after. But listen to this – the best thing was when she left after three glasses of wine – about midnight, I think. She took hold of my shoulders and gave me a little shake and said very seriously that if Roland tried to reignite our marriage I must not take him back, not for any reason, she made me promise. Like she was talking to a slightly unreliable child. So funny!'

25

When Ossie the Aussie, the man she had met at Baluga, texted and invited her for a drink, and said how much he and Cilla had enjoyed meeting her, she accepted because a couple of new friends would be nice as a distraction from feeling more or less constantly either sad or for some reason worried about the trip north. The little bistro, which Ossie called 'one of our fave hangouts', was a place she had never heard of before, but again it sounded nice.

Amy pulled the door open and came to a sudden halt when she picked up that unnerving scent of hot oil. Instead of walking further in she scanned the bar and the area to one side, a recessed room with four tables, but Simon wasn't there and neither did she recognise the man from the train. Then an arm was raised further back, and she realised Ossie was sitting alone at a small round table for two against the far wall, which was odd, but maybe Cilla was in the restroom or coming along later.

'Hi, Ossie! Is Cilla not here yet?' The hot oil smell was stronger here and warning bells rang in Amy's head. She slid her jacket off and hung it on the back of her chair. 'Are we meeting Pete and Roger here?'

Ossie looked slightly taken aback and said, 'Pete and Roger? No, they're not part of this.'

'Oh – well, never mind. I don't know why I thought they would be here,' said Amy, who had thought no such thing but was testing the waters, because there was something slightly off about this. 'But where's Cilla then?'

I hope this isn't what I think it might be, she thought, or I'll just get up and leave. That damn oil smell is very strong here, very strange that I didn't get it when I met him the first time, this isn't a good idea at all.

'It's just you and me getting to know each other a bit better – quite a bit better, I hope.' Ossie smiled across the little table and the look on his face was one she knew well. 'What can I get you to drink?'

'Nothing, thanks.' Amy got to her feet, plucked her jacket from the back of the chair and walked through the room and out the door without looking back. She turned at the first corner to make sure he wasn't following her then hailed a passing cab.

As soon as she had given the driver her address she got her phone out and called Pete. 'What a devious prick!' he exclaimed when she had told him what just happened. 'I'm sorry you met him through us. I had no idea he was that type, but we haven't known him long. Cilla and I worked together a few years ago and we've just reconnected. So what did you do?'

Amy grinned to herself. 'I just left – I didn't say goodbye or anything, I just walked out and left him sitting there all on his lonesome, and now I'm in a cab on the way home.'

'Come over here then, have supper with us! Roger has cooked something new, a Moroccan thing in a special pottery casserole he bought and there seems to be loads of it. Just change your destination and join us.'

Twenty minutes later Pete to open the door to the penthouse and the smell of exotic spices flowed out. Roger, equipped with two oven gloves, was just putting a tagine on the table and Amy felt instantly happy and ravenous in equal parts. 'God, that smells delicious – I'm starving. This is such a treat!'

Roger lifted the conical lid off the tagine and revealed the simmering contents, a mass of orange and yellow with pieces of meat poking through here and there. 'Lamb and lots of ingredients,' he said proudly. 'Eleven spices, dates and almonds and lots more, and it smells great, doesn't it?'

'You're a marvel, Roger.' Amy smiled and thought how lucky this was, catching up with these two and a fabulous meal. 'You can't imagine how cross I was when I walked out of that bistro. And disappointed, because I really liked Cilla when I met her with you. The cheek of the man – asking me out without saying it would only be him and me. The way he put it in the message gave me no clue. But that hot oil smell, it hit me the moment I went in the door, so I was kind of prepared.'

'Hot oil smell? Please explain – I think I've missed something,' said Pete. Both men were looking strangely at her and she suddenly realised that maybe it was not just Kate who didn't know about the phenomenon they had decided to call the smell signature. Perhaps a lot of people didn't. And why had she blurted out the smell thing like that, anyway? Not something she'd usually mention.

'You know - that thing that happens now and then,' she said and watched Roger put twice as much food as she normally ate on her plate. 'With me it only happens with men – I think of it as the smell signature. And for me the smell of overheated cooking oil means a certain type of man is close by – I used to think it was just Simon, but lately I've discovered it's not specific to him.'

Confused, Roger stared at her with the plate still in his hand, and Pete regarded her with a hint of hidden laughter. 'Smell signature? Are you having us on? You can smell men?' He paused. 'I mean, not as in aftershave or soap but like some kind of … aura?'

'I used to think everyone did until I mentioned it

to my friend Kate. She doesn't get it and says she's never heard about it. She thought I was trying to trick her, but it's real.'

The men exchanged a look that made Amy laugh – a look of disbelief from one and concern from the other. She decided to say nothing about Kate's research just now and just wait. After a long moment of silence, Roger put her plate in front of her and said calmly while he served Pete, 'This is possibly the weirdest thing anyone's ever said to me, but as opposed to Pete, who clearly doesn't believe you, I do – however mad it seems. You have to tell us more because you obviously can't smell every man you meet – is it random?'

'I thought maybe men would get the smell signature with women,' said Amy slowly. 'Not that I've ever thought of it before now, but it seems reasonable, doesn't it? I've always assumed I get it only in regard to men because it's kind of like an early warning once you decode the smells. Like with Simon – you know how controlling and nasty he could be, Pete. He was the first one who gave me that sensation of smelling overheated oil. But recently it's expanded to strangers, like a guy on the train the other day. I smelt that horrid stink and looked around, thinking it might be Simon, who had a tracking app on my phone, so he could turn up wherever I went after I broke up with him. But anyway, Simon wasn't on the train, but this total stranger was staring at me, and it was obvious the smell was coming from him – the look on his face told me all I needed to know.'

Once again total silence followed, and Amy, who knew she had taken a risk by being open about this, helped herself to rice and started eating her dinner and said with her mouth full, 'My God, Roger, this is delicious! Top class – can I come for dinner more often please?'

She continued eating and waited for some comment, any sort of response really, but the silence prevailed, and after a minute or two she lost her patience. 'Could you two please stop sitting there staring and making me feel like I'm a freak and say something?'

'It's unbelievable,' said Pete slowly. 'I can see you're serious and it's real - to start with I thought it was one of your naughty jokes, trying to trick me. I've never heard about anything like it, not ever. It's like something out of a science fiction novel. Has this been with you since childhood?'

'Oh no, it never happened until I was adult. It started after I was in that bike crash – remember our first year at university when a car knocked me off my bike and I got a bad concussion? You used to come and keep me company while I wasn't allowed to go out for a couple of weeks. You were the first to have a smell signature – lemon grass. I only worked out when it first started quite recently after telling Kate about it. Looking back, I could pinpoint it, and you were the first.'

Another moment of silence while Pete and

Roger exchanged another glance, but neither of them said nothing.

'What?' said Amy. 'For God's sake, what's wrong *now*?'

'It's just so surprising – lemon grass! Fabulous scent, but how did you know it wasn't my aftershave?'

Amy laughed because this conversation was becoming both interesting and unexpectedly funny and exploring this strange talent of hers with trusted friends was good.

'Oh, I didn't – not to start with. But then I realised that some men have this signature smell and it's always the same, yours is lemon grass, Roger doesn't have one, the guy on the train stank of hot oil and Ben ...'

'Ah, Ben ... what does he smell of?'

'Cinnamon – but I don't want to talk about him. I might cry if I do. I've never told anybody about this, aside from Kate, and I'd never thought of it in any detail until recently.' She took a deep breath. 'Not all men have a signature smell, but those who do are either a threat – hot oil – or they are fond of me or attracted to me, or they're affectionate friends."

Roger frowned. 'And I don't have a smell? But I like you, I really do.'

'You're probably too new in my life and you're not a threat. If you really do like me a smell will turn up, I'm sure. We've probably just got to give it time. Perhaps it will be this tagine smell – what could be better?' She smiled and hoped she had diverted them away from asking about Ben. 'And I've only just this second realised – my dad doesn't have a smell and neither does my boss, Stefan. But George, our receptionist, does - he smells of cloves. How odd that I've never thought of it before that some men, who I know like me and I feel close to, don't have a smell!'

Towards midnight, after ice cream with crushed roasted walnuts sprinkled over it and a conversation that meandered between subjects without structure, Amy got up to go.

'Thank you both! This has been such a lovely evening, and I'm so grateful I didn't have to return home full of indignation after the Ossie debacle with no one to listen to the story.'

'You know that signature smell thing – I've been sure all evening that it reminded me of something, and I've just got it,' said Roger. 'It's a novel I read last year, a story about a woman who got concussed and then started seeing colours wash in front of her eyes when people's thoughts related to her – *and* she heard their thoughts like spoken words in her mind. And the colour was always the same for each person, like a signature. Great story! Maybe it's something that only happens after concussions – to certain people?'

'Paranormal fiction?' Pete laughed. 'Really, Roger? You're reading paranormal novels now, about women?'

'God, no! Don't be silly – not my thing at all. No,

it was a romantic novel – hetero for a change. I'll find it on my Kindle and text you the name so you can read it too, you really should, Amy.'

She had Roger's message on her phone before she got home: *It's called The Colour of Love – very good story. About a woman mechanic. Rxx*

26

<hr>

The text from Kate was mysterious, not say confusing: 'Change of plan for Saturday. Take the tube to Mornington Crescent and exit on Eversholt Street. 11 am, I'll be outside. There's something you've got to see – it includes lunch, my treat. Don't be late. K'

After staring amazed at this message and not able to make any kind of sense of it, Amy responded, 'Intrigued! I'll be there. A'

What she really wanted to say was, 'What on earth is this about and can you please tell me some more?' or perhaps 'Would you like me to try to guess what you're up to?' but somehow the tone of that message made it clear that no questions would be answered. She thought about it on and off during the day and came to the conclusion that Kate was taking her to some place she had recently discovered, probably a particularly gorgeous café.

But anything Kate suggested was likely to be intriguing and interesting and something Amy had never come across before, so she looked forward to finding out what it was.

On the Friday night she checked the weather forecast. Not that she knew how far she would have to walk on this mysterious date with Kate, but it seemed sensible at this time of the year, and particularly during this awful autumn when it rained nearly all the time, and strong winds made even a light shower nearly drenching. The forecast was moderately good, but on the Saturday morning she put on her storm jacket that buttoned right up to her chin and with a hood that pulled tight around her face, just in case it did rain more than predicted. With her mane of thick hair, it was better to be overly careful than having to sit through lunch with damp hair on her shoulders.

At ten past eleven, she came up onto Eversholt Street to light rain, pulled the hood up and spotted Kate, also dressed in a sensible coat and wearing a sombrero style rainhat.

'Let's start walking right away,' she said after greeting Amy. 'We've got to be there before half past.'

'Where are we going? We're not going to the movies are we?' Not that Amy could imagine why they would go to see a film at half past eleven in the morning, or why they were in this strange location, where there were probably no movie theatres anyway. But what else had a deadline that had to be met in the middle of the day?

'Wait and see,' was all the reply she got, and the look Katee gave her, that sideways slanting look with a quirked eyebrow, told her that asking questions was pointless and no answers would be forthcoming.

'Here we are.' Kate put a hand on Amy's arm and steered her toward the steps up to the main door of a church on a corner. 'Come along!'

What a strange location for a church, right on a corner with an office building practically sharing a wall, thought Amy and glanced up at the dark stonework. I've never been on this street before. I hope I'm not here to lend her my support at a funeral, maybe I should have worn a dark coat and not this bright yellow jacket.

'Perfect timing!' said a voice she knew well, and there was Patrick in a dark suit and white shirt, looking impossibly handsome. Amy stared while her brain rapidly computed the facts: church, gentle organ music, dark suit, Kate removing her coat and revealing a beautiful pale blue silk tunic over dark trousers. Stunned she watched Patrick hand Kate a pair of black high heels and looked from one to the other, speechless, while they silently looked back, both of them amused and expectant in equal parts.

'Surprise, surprise!' Patrick reached for her with both hands and pulled her into a hug. 'We're getting married, and you're one of our two witnesses, well,

I suppose you're the bridesmaid or something. The other witness will be here soon. He just texted that he's in a cab and nearly here.'

Amy burst out laughing, this was the most surprising thing that had happened to her for years, possibly ever. 'I can't believe it - you're actually doing it and in a church! A real wedding! And isn't it lucky I'm wearing nice pants instead of jeans?'

She was just about to ask who the second witness was when he arrived. A tall thin man with a dour, deeply lined face, who looked vaguely familiar, was pulling off his coat as he approached, ready it to drape it over the back of the pew alongside Kate's and Amy's coats.

'Amy, this is Dougal, my cousin,' said Patrick. 'The only person apart from us two who knew about this from the very start, because he had to come a lot further than everyone else - well, not counting the vicar of course, he knew too. Ah yes, and there he is now, so let's walk up the aisle together and let him do his job.'

Amy looked at Kate, who smiled calmly, and put her hand on Patrick's arm. 'You are without a doubt a very sly person, not to say secretive! That mysterious message telling me where to come! I knew it was pointless trying to make you tell me more, but *this* I would never have guessed.'

Not until they were halfway up the aisle did Amy notice that there were twenty or perhaps thirty people seated in the pews closest to the front, who now rose to watch the informal bridal procession approach. With Dougal and Amy standing slightly to one side the priest started the service in the time honoured manner: 'Dearly beloved, we are here today to unite Kate and Patrick in holy matrimony ...' and from there the brief service proceeded smoothly. Patrick fished a ring out of his pocket and put it on Kate's finger and it was done.

Outside and in a disjointed fashion with people crowding around Patrick and Kate, they introduced their guests to each other. Patrick's parents and his younger brother Mark, an uncle and aunt and a couple of cousins and at least fifteen people on Kate's side, including her twin sisters Amy had never heard about before. Everyone took photos of the newly married couple on the steps outside the church with Kate standing one step higher than Patrick, so she didn't look quite so short in comparison. A passer-by was roped in to take some shots of the entire group of guests, an exercise which took several minutes to orchestrate, with endless instructions from the woman holding the phone for someone to move slightly more to the left or right. Just as the rain started falling again three minibus taxis pulled up, and Patrick's father, who had a loud booming voice, made himself heard over the chatter and laughter and told everyone to get on board.

· · ·

At Covent Garden the minibus taxis stopped, everyone streamed in, talking and laughing and without having time to look around properly, Amy was absorbed into a group of Patrick's relations.

'Did you have any idea what you were coming to witness?' asked Amy of Patrick's brother, Mark, who was seated next to her at one of the two long tables. 'I had no idea at all!'

'The two families were told a week ago.' He grinned. 'I suppose they had to make sure we could all come – but we hadn't met Kate until this morning. Isn't she sweet?'

Amy thought how surprised he would be when he got to know Kate better and said, 'There's a lot more to Kate than being sweet – which she is, of course. She's very clever and possibly the best person I've ever met if you want advice about something – and I mean advice about *anything*. She's my go-to friend for good advice.'

Mark looked across the table at Patrick and Kate and shook his head as in disbelief. 'I never thought he'd get married, and I would never have expected him to marry someone like Kate. No offence intended but just look at the height difference!'

Into Amy's mind came to image of Ben, built like a cliff, a head taller than her, and her heart clenched with regret and sadness, but before she could think of a reply Patrick got to his feet and tapped his glass with a spoon.

'Kate and I want to thank you all for coming,' he said and looked down at Kate who smiled up at him. 'This wedding would never have happened if it hadn't been for Amy, who's sitting next to Mark just there. She introduced us and it all developed rapidly after a first dinner together followed by coffee at her place. Kate and I knew within minutes that we were two of a kind with many shared interests, and despite the fact that Kate is an avid reader, and I never read fiction, we knew very soon that we were made to be together. Here's a toast to Amy who introduced us, and to all of you for coming along today - and to us!'

Two hours later when everyone was moving around and swapping seats, Patrick pulled Amy aside to sit on a banquette at one side of the room.

'I need to fill you in, I think. It was that comment of mine at your place,' he said quietly. 'You know how I nearly proposed to Kate, suggested she could be my camouflage bride? And then I got so embarrassed that I nearly sank though the floor. Well, we met up the next day and the day after and then again and again – and this is the result. And no, I can see the question on your face, most of these people have never heard the term asexual and would have no idea what it means. Only you, Kate and I know the real background.'

'Incredible, isn't it?' Kate had appeared on the far side of Patrick and was leaning across to look at Amy. 'It seemed like it was meant to be. We liked each other a lot from the very start, and we're both pretty much asexual, so it's the perfect arrangement. And Patrick's flat is far nicer than mine and *much* bigger and smarter, so we'll have lots of space to be on our own if we feel like it.'

She smiled at Amy and turned to Dougal who had sat down beside Amy. 'I've got Barbara's phone – that's Patrick's mum, Amy. Let's have a look at those photos she took of us with Amy and you on the church steps. We've got to pick a couple that only show our top halves of course, so people can't see that I'm standing one step higher. We don't want to look silly.'

'Are you going to post it on social media? And will your agency spread it far and wide, Patrick?' Amy, who didn't know how much Dougal knew about the reason behind this marriage, tried to be discrete, but she really wanted to know.

'Both. I've got thousands of followers on Instagram so the reach should be impressive, and my agent's asked for photos to put on their website.' They smiled at each other and said no more.

Over the next few days Amy followed the news of Patrick's wedding both in the papers and on social media and smiled every time she saw the photo of the four of them on the church steps, with the newly married couple in the middle and herself and Dougal flanking them, all of them smiling widely. When she texted Patrick and asked why Dougal seemed vaguely familiar his reply made her giggle to herself. 'He's the minister for social services in Scotland, so you've probably seen his photo.' She recalled the stories Dougal had told, and the sly and slightly risqué parts of his speech to the newly married couple – everything about that dour looking man was unexpected, not least that he was handsome Patrick's cousin.

27

On the day Amy was catching the train to what she called the far north, which was in fact only Newcastle, she spent most of the day working online from home, tidying up the last details of a report to the Stock Exchange, and then decided to walk to Kings Cross. It was a perfect afternoon with the sun shining and little wind and walking briskly would keep her warm. She hitched the laptop bag over her shoulder, picked up her light overnight bag and thought she would be able to cover the distance in plenty of time before her train left. She set out along the towpath beside the canal, feeling slightly more positive about the prospect of the Newcastle visit. It might turn out to be interesting, at least the prospect of being more or less undercover, which Jordan Marsh had explained over the phone a couple of days ago.

'How is this going to work?' Amy had asked him,

with a niggling worry that his idea of getting her into the workplace was fraught with problems, some of them probably highly embarrassing. 'I'm bringing an SSD hard drive so I can copy everything, but I do hope your business partner really will be away or he'll get suspicious. I'll be glued to a computer in full view for a few hours, possibly longer if I have problems.'

'No, Martin's away now and he doesn't come back until next week. It's his twenty-fifth wedding anniversary and they flew to Paris last night. I've told the admin manager and our internal accountant that you're coming to assess if we can afford to have new software designed to integrate our various systems a bit better. You're officially a tech guru and specialist software designer.'

She thought for a moment, keen to get this sorted out in her mind, because up to now she hadn't realised they had an internal accountant, the very person who might smell a rat and start asking inconvenient questions.

'I'll have to go into your bank records as well – that's where the real evidence will be even if you couldn't see it when you started looking. We'll probably do what we call a data crunch to pull it all together.'

She heard Jordan's quiet chuckle and continued, 'Don't worry, we're not actually going to crunch anything – it's a silly phrase we use in situations like yours. I'll have to analyse data from your direct credit schedules, your internal accounting software and the bank transactions.'

'OK, but can you do that in the time you'll be here? Or do you need to stay a bit longer?'

'I'll get it done in one day, I think. Do you know if you have an audit trail of user logons on your server? It would prove whose logon was used for various things, like creating fake creditors and changed account numbers for payments, that kind of thing.'

'I haven't a clue, but I'll find out. I can see that would be a great thing – unless Martin's deleted the trail as you call it.'

'If it's on the server it should be out of his reach, only accessible by IT maintenance people – for a very good reason, as I'm sure you can understand.'

'Totally!' said Jordan. 'God, I hope we have it – it would be like leaving fingerprints, wouldn't it?'

'Yes, very useful, but listen, I hope the accountant isn't going to become suspicious,' said Amy. 'Won't they want to have an input into this supposed IT upgrade plan of yours?'

'She doesn't seem in the least suspicious. She's been on at us for a year or more to rationalise things – she says she's sick of having to transfer things from various spreadsheets to produce her monthly reports, so she can't wait for you to arrive.' He chuckled. 'It was only this morning she said how convenient it is that you can come just this week when Martin's away. He's the one who's argued against her demands. Not that *she* suspects why he's so against it, but that doesn't matter.'

He was definitely amused by how well the deception was working, thought Amy and began to feel a bit more confident about the whole venture. 'I suppose Martin said it would be too expensive or something, so that's the official reason he's against it and your accountant believed it.'

'Yes, exactly. Sonia, that's our accountant, she'll be very helpful – she wants this project underway as soon as possible.'

'Does she realise Martin wants to put the company into liquidation? Has he ever said you should put it under administration instead?'

Jordan's voice was noticeably harder when he replied, and Amy could hear how furious he was with his partner. 'No, we've kept it between us two. He says we can't recover, and he wants it liquidated, and that we can't afford to borrow any more money to get back on track, it's too risky – but it's only so he can get out without the company being declared bankrupt. He's trying to avoid being tagged as a neglectful director, of course. Sonia doesn't know this yet, so be careful what you say to her. She thinks we're going to raise some capital to carry us over this period until we're back in the black. And …'

He paused and Amy waited, certain there was something else on his mind. After a few moments he continued, sounding more troubled now. 'I think he's beginning to wonder if I'm onto him. We're not communicating as easily as we used to.'

'I'm not surprised,' said Amy who found this statement surprisingly naïve. 'If you've been arguing about this and you now also suspect him of fraud, he'd sense it for sure. Does he actually think he can close the business down and then live on whatever he's stolen? Is he that stupid?'

'Cunning but not clever,' said Jordan dismissively, and there the conversation ended.

Now Amy enjoyed her walk along the towpath, but she stopped halfway to switch her laptop bag to the other shoulder and took the opportunity to check the time and saw she still had plenty of time. By the time she got to Coal Drop Yard she was getting hot in her warm coat but taking it off and carrying it wasn't an option. She thought longingly of the café where she had sat with Pete and Roger earlier in the autumn and the lovely, chilled fruit smoothie she had ordered, just what she could do with right now. She climbed the steps from the towpath to the walkway and continued on her way. What a wonderful environment this was, the blend of history and modern business, the canal with greenery on the far side and the longboats tied up here and there. But how many Londoners ever walked along the canal or knew the background to these old buildings? She must do this walk with her dad one weekend, if she could drag him away from his busy life. He would enjoy this, and maybe Kirsten would like to meet her here some time too. Recurring thoughts of Kirsten and occasional text messages were part of her everyday life now in a way she could never have anticipated when she first decided to have her DNA analysed – a lovely addition to her life.

By the time she was seated in a comfortable window seat and the train slowly moved out from the station she felt relieved, even if the forecast was for snow in the north. A change of scene and doing something different from her daily routine was something to look forward to. Not quite an adventure, but a couple of days with new experiences.

Her mood, which had been briefly lifted by the surprising wedding, had soon slumped again once she was back in her flat after the celebration lunch. She had spent a lot of time wondering how Patrick and Kate's arrangement had been worked out. Which one had first raised the possibility of a marriage of convenience as a serious prospect, not just a casual joke? Had they worked out how their daily life would be organised, or were they leaving things to develop organically? Hopefully Kate would tell her at least some of it at their next lunch date, because she really wanted to know. The whole idea was intriguing, and Amy wondered if she could include it in a future book. Perhaps she could use it as a secondary plot, something running alongside the main story line to provide an unusual flavour.

Not until the train was well out of London did it occur to her that there was now no certainty that her weekend dates with Kate would continue, but after a few moments she decided it seemed unlikely that Kate would change how she lived her life, apart from perhaps joining in with Patrick's social life. The whole intention was, after all, to give him a normal married life.

28

When Amy arrived at the North Wind factory she was surprised at how large it was and how impressive. For a company making what their website described as small scale wind turbines for businesses and homes the size of the factory seemed out of proportion. The receptionist was friendly and had been told to expect Amy, got to her feet and came around her desk to shake hands.

'Welcome! I'm Marybelle - come with me and I'll show you were to go,' she said and started walking down a corridor to the left. 'How was your hotel? I booked you there because it's supposed to be better than most of the others.' Then she laughed and added, 'Not that I know for a fact – it's not as if you stay in hotels in your own city, is it?'

'It's very good and I had exactly the kind of breakfast I like, which isn't always possible with breakfasts buffets.'

'Oh, what did you have?'

'Wholemeal toast with peanut butter, the crunchy kind, and coffee. And the coffee was great and hadn't been sitting on a hotplate. It was made on the spot with a huge Italian coffee machine.'

'Excellent! Here's Sonia's office. She's on the phone but just go in and sit down, she's expecting you.'

Surprising, thought Amy and sat down in the chair across from Sonia's desk while she nodded and smiled, and then continued making notes while she listened. I thought I'd see Jordan first, so this must mean something's changed.

A couple of minutes lates Sonia put the phone down, pushed her notepad aside and got up to shake hands. 'Sorry about this - Jordan wanted to be here to greet you, but he's going to be late. His son broke his ankle this morning, but he he'll be here by lunchtime. Tell me what you want to start with – I'm not sure exactly how this process will work. I imagine you want to see how our so-called system works and why it's so unwieldy?'

A growing sense of something wrong had filtered into Amy's mind while Sonia was speaking. Was Somia worried that Amy would find fault with how she had done things so far, or was it something personal? Half an hour later, after sitting side by side in front of Sonia's computer as she went through the various data sources she had to link and cobble together to get a full picture, Amy was sure she was right.

'Is something wrong?' she asked casually. 'I hope you don't feel I'm here to pick holes in your work and how you do it? Quite the opposite, in fact.'

There was a long silence while Sonia looked down at the keyboard in front of her. Amy could feel her hesitation like a physical sensation, then Sonia looked up and spoke very fast, as if she wanted to get it out before she changed her mind.

'I'm worried, have been for some time. Something's very wrong with our financial results. And maybe you'll come across something when you start working on this project, something that alerts you, so I think I'd better tell you. I don't know who's doing it and I can't prove it, because I can't figure out how it's done – but I think money is being syphoned off. Big money, and when I look back I'm sure it's been going on for a while. It's not a one- off thing, or I would have found it. It must have been going on for some time.'

She looked anguished, as if telling Amy had been nearly more than she could bear, and Amy was just about to reply when Sonia added, 'And I'm really worried it will be blamed on me somehow, some time in the future – if I'm right.'

It only took a moment for Amy to decide she had to be frank because this woman was worried both about the company and herself, an unfair situation to leave her in after she had the courage to bring it up.

'That's the reason I'm here,' she said calmly. 'Jordan knows about the money disappearing, and he's called me in to help. I'm not here to construct a new system for you, I'm a forensic accountant and I'm here to find out how it's been done, gather a lot of data and do what we flippantly call a data crunch – you might have heard the expression.'

'Oh, thank God! I've been so worried, you can't imagine – lying awake at night and trying to decide if my instincts are right and who I should tell. When I heard you were coming I wondered if it was some kind of manoeuvre to conceal evidence, kind of delete it from the records.' She gave Amy a tremulous smile. 'But Jordan sounded so genuine I decided I must have been wrong, and it was just an opportunity to pull all our systems together into some kind of order.' She paused and added, 'And I didn't think it could be him – he's a nice, honest guy and he's been having terrible arguments with Martin. You could hear them all over the building, Martin shouting and swearing.'

Half an hour later they had set themselves up in Sonia's office in a way that would make the process easier, Sonia on her computer and Amy on her laptop with one of North Wind's laptops beside it, using Sonia's logon.

'We back up on the cloud each night. I can access backed up data remotely, but I can't change anything in the cloud of course. I sometimes wonder where it is, could be in some data centre in Lapland. Let's go and get ourselves some coffee, and

I'll make some notes about what you just said, so I know what I need to ask IGL about that audit trail for logons. I'd never heard of it before, but if it's there it would be beyond price now! And I'm not sure if they can access it.'

'You won't need to go to the cloud backup for that – we'll get it off your server here in the building. If IGL is the tech company that looks after your systems, we'll ask them – I can talk to them if you like. But we have to find out how it was done first, checking whose logon was used is the final step of detection work.'

Sonia looked a lot more cheerful and relaxed now, and Amy thought she might even get to enjoy this process of discovery, appreciate it like a detective story. 'When people steal from an employer or from their own company for some reason they usually go about it in one of three or four ways, so we'll just work through the obvious option first.' Amy pushed her chair back and smiled at Sonia. 'Let's get that coffee now and then we'll start.'

'Ok,' she said ten minutes later. 'First we'll go through your creditors and your direct credit schedules for the bank and to see what changes have been made in the last couple of years. If there's a way of checking that without any detours our job will be much easier. Then we look at all new creditors to see if they are real companies, and if they are real we call them and doublecheck what their bank account numbers are. Entering a new creditor and using another bank account for payments to go to is possible if the thief has found out how to do it without alerting the banks. I believe there's a kind of thief's manual on the dark web that tells you how to do it.'

When Jordan turned up at lunchtime, full of apologies, he was surprised to find them working side by side in Sonia's office with three computers open. Amy could see his hesitation, so she took the lead.

'You'll be pleased to hear that your accountant is as sharp as you are,' she said lightly. 'She's been having the exactly the same suspicions you have, that considerable sums of money must have disappeared for the results to have changed so radically without any obvious reason.'

She made no mention of what Jordan had told her about his partner wanting to declare a voluntary bankruptcy or something similar, and hopefully there would be no need for Sonia to know this. After a moment of silence while he digested this Jordan smiled at Sonia. 'You have no idea what a relief it is to hear this! I knew it wasn't you, but I didn't feel I could talk about it until Amy had done her work. What are you two doing now?'

Sonia returned his smile, relaxed and confident now. 'We're going through the background stuff now, and then Amy will pull things together for her analysis. And I'll get IGL to get some data from our server here in the office – and then we'll see. But I shouldn't be the one telling you how it's going to work! Amy can do it much better.'

'You've just about covered it.' Amy tapped her finger on her pad, already full of scribbled notes. 'We'll possibly have a better idea before the end of today and then I'll document what we found tomorrow. Either here or back in my office in London. But there are no guarantees it will be that quick – depends on how sophisticated the thief has been.'

Jordan's expression told her he understood why she put it that way and he nodded. 'OK, I'll let you get on with it and I'll be available if you need to talk to me. I've kept today and tomorrow clear.'

'And how is your son?' Amy remembered to ask just as he turned to go to his own office. 'I'm sorry, I should have asked earlier - is he OK?"

'Lying on his bed playing games on his laptop, his leg is in a cast and his mother has taken the week off. She knows why you're here and that I have to be here.' His smile was slightly smug, as if he congratulated himself on not having to take responsibility for his son's recuperation, thought Amy, then told herself not to be judgmental and returned to the task in front of her.

Over a late lunch with Jordan and Sonia in their meeting room Amy remembered her thought from early that morning when she first arrived at the plant. 'I was surprised at the size of this place when I arrived – much bigger than I had expected. You could build passenger jets here.'

'Chance and circumstance,' said Jordan. 'When we built it there was a shortage of factory spaces for rent that were tall enough for large gantry cranes, so we built big and rent out the far end, the bigger end, to a company making steel framing for buildings. Their entrance is from the road behind us. But if we get over this trouble and look for more export opportunities we might have to get rid of the tenant or build an extension. Fingers crossed.'

By midafternoon Amy's pad was beginning to look promising with two scam creditors added in the last two years and five doubtful ones to be investigated further.

'Right!' said Amy. 'Let's map out how it will work from here. We check those last five suspect creditors, then we'll print all payments to confirmed fake creditors along with their bank account numbers and the relevant invoice numbers. Then we find the physical invoices and check who signed them off for payment. We'll also record when each of those creditors was entered into your system. Then we'll check if any payments to those creditors were made aside from your routine credit schedule – like if one of them was paid just by itself, perhaps unexpectedly. When we're satisfied we've got every single detail, we'll go to the logon audit trail on your inhouse server and check whose logon was used to enter those creditors into the system and we'll have our thief.'

Sonia leaned back in her chair and unexpectedly burst out laughing. 'This is incredible! I should have thought of doing a bit of more to find out what was going on myself, but you've made it so clear and simple – it's like being a detective. But why check who signed off the fake invoices for payment if we can show how entered those fake suppliers into the system?'

As always Amy had that feeling of deep satisfaction, the internal *Yes!* when things started falling into place and a pattern started to emerge. 'This is probably the simplest way to steal, definitely the most common one. It just takes time to work through everything and document the findings. There are far more sophisticated ways of stealing, but whoever did this probably chose the most straightforward method. And it could be that two people are involved – which is why we check who signed off fake invoices.'

She drank some of her water and contemplated asking Sonia if she had a theory and in that case what it was and had just decided against it when Sonia said quite casually. 'I know who it must be. If it isn't Jordan, which it can't be, or he wouldn't have called you in then it's got to be Martin. Those two and I are the only ones who can enter new suppliers. They have the right kind of access, and I showed them how to do it a couple of years ago when I had to be away after cancer surgery. They didn't want my temporary replacement to do that. The admin staff and the foreman can't do it.'

They looked at each other for a long moment without comment and went back to their tasks.

By the end of Amy's second day at North Wind the list of scam creditors had grown to six, which as she said, might seem a considerable number, but as a portion of over one hundred and fifty suppliers was not excessive and easy to miss. She backed up all the evidence including photos of a selection of signed off invoices on her external hard drive and saved it on her laptop and promised to provide a report within a couple of days.

'Excellent,' said Jordan. 'That means I can organise a full audit and report it to the police or however this is going to work. I'll have to check with our solicitor, but it must be underway before Martin gets back. What time does your train leave? I'll take you to the station.'

'I'm book on the half past seven train, so I'll just hang around here. My bag 's in Sonia's office, so I'll start writing the report now seeing I've got another hour and a half. I'll take a taxi so you can both get home.'

'No way,' said Sonia. 'We can raid the fridge and have some snacks and a glass of wine while you write the report, and then I'll take you to the station. It's my privilege after all you've taught me –

I've never been involved in anything to interesting before!'

29

Not long before the train reached Darlington came an announcement that made everyone take notice; head turned as people exchanged glances and comments of dismay.

"Due to unexpectedly heavy snowfall between Darlington and York this service will stop for half an hour at Darlington to await further developments. At the moment the snow is unlikely to cause a problem. A further update will be broadcast as soon as we know more. We ask passengers not leave the train at Darlington, as we might be able to resume our journey sooner than expected, so the delay might be shorter than half an hour."

'This can't be happening!' The young man in the seat next to Amy sounded close to panic. 'I can't afford to be late. It could ruin everything.'

For a moment Amy considered if simply ignoring this dramatic exclamation was the kindest thing to do so as not to embarrass him, but she noticed out of the corner of her eye that he had turned to look at her. Maybe some slightly optimistic comment will make him feel better, she thought, and turned to meet his agonised gaze.

'They always exaggerate about these delays,' she lied calmly, as if she was a frequent train traveller and knew how things worked. 'They always say half an hour or even longer, and then they spend two minutes stopped somewhere before it's OK to move again.'

'Do they?' said the young man hopefully and attempted a smile that didn't quite get off the ground. 'I hope you're right! Everything depends on this job I'm after in York. It's the second interview and there are only two of us left to choose from – it's vital that I get it.'

'Tell me about the job. Is it important because it's a step up or is the pay really good? Or maybe both?' Keep him talking, she thought and studied the tense line of his lips. The poor guy is genuinely worried, maybe talking about it might calm him down.

'Very important for my career. *And* it would give me an opportunity to be closer to my girlfriend. But I think it's doomed now. I couldn't get the earlier train, and my appointment is only half an hour after we're supposed to arrive in York – just enough time to get there by taxi.'

'An interview in the evening? That's unusual. Why is it at night and what kind of job is it?'

'I'm in IT security development – well, not quite, but that's what the job is about, and I really want to get it. Lots of scope for future advancement, not to mention how interesting that area of IT is. It's the best opportunity I've had after four or five years in programming. They're doing my interview tonight because I couldn't get there any sooner, and the HR woman is on leave from tomorrow! This is a real fuck-up! Sorry!'

The conversation dwindled to nothing when Amy failed to think of anything helpful to ask or say and a short while later the train stopped at Darlington. After a few minutes there was a deep sigh from beside her and she could feel his increased level of worry as a change of air pressure.

'What's your name? I'm Amy,' she said, but the reply she got was a brief, 'Thomas.' She noticed his left hand clenched into a fist on his thigh and was tempted to reach out that and put her hand on his, but of course she didn't, it would have been totally inappropriate, and he might take it the wrong way. When fifteen minutes had passed Thomas said on a note of despondency, 'That's it. I'll never make it now.'

Amy didn't reply because her mind was busy trying to come up with a solution, and then as suddenly as if someone had flicked a switch, there it was, the idea that might resolve the problem.

'Here's a thought - maybe a bit unconventional, but beggars can't be choosers, and it's worth trying. You could call that HR manager and tell her you're stuck on a train, and you won't get there on time, and could you please do the interview via FaceTime or WhatsApp or whatever kind of thing they can organise. Surely everyone has one of those on their phone.'

Thomas stared at her with doubt written all over his face. 'Do you think she'd really agree to that?'

'Why not? You're one of two final candidates, so you must have the qualifications and the qualities they want, so why wouldn't she? And now that so many have got off the train there's lots of room. You can sit over on the other side where there are several empty seats, so you get some privacy. Surely it's better than giving up?'

After a long silence while Thomas continued to look at her with creases between his ginger eyebrows he said, 'You're right - what have I got to lose? It's better than just giving up, isn't it?' He got his phone out. 'I'll find her phone number now - it will be in the footer of the e-mail they sent about this appointment.'

To avoid embarrassing him, Amy got up and went to the toilet, and by the time she returned Thomas was beaming. 'You won't believe it! They've given me the job without the second interview – the other candidate backed out for some reason.' Then he laughed quietly and said, 'The HR woman said if it had been up to her she would have hired me without any interview at all because of my name.'

Amy could tell something funny was coming up, and seeing his freckly face with a smile was such a treat after all the agonising he had gone through. 'Your name? You'll have to fill me in.'

'My full name is Thomas Edison would you believe. It was always turned into jokes at school, and I used to curse my parents. But this HR woman I just talked to thinks it's great.'

Twenty minutes later there was another announcement telling them that they would be moving within a few minutes, that the brief snowstorm seemed to have passed and their arrival in York would be fifty-four minutes later than scheduled.

By the time they left Darlington the tracks no longer followed a road and Amy could see nothing, not even car headlights, through the window, only a reflection of her face, but she felt unsettled and kept glancing out anyway. In the back of her mind her conversation with Stefan about blizzards kept reminding her that she could have flown and been home by now, safe from delays and uncertainty. When the train slowed again she looked at Thomas, who seemed oblivious of any potential threat, and he looked up from his phone.

'It's probably the place where there was a lot of snow on the track,' he said calmly. 'I suppose they go slowly if they have to push a lot of stuff off the rails.'

Though she felt embarrassed by how obvious her worry must have been, she was grateful for his calm reassurance. 'It's your turn now,' she said with a wry smile. 'Now I'm the anxious one.'

'Well, thank you for your support earlier– you made me feel a lot better! It's been a good team effort.' He looked around. 'I think I'll go and sit over where I was when I talked to the HR woman and call my girlfriend.'

To Amy his devotion to his girlfriend made her think of Ben and how she wished she could call him and tell him she was worried about being on a train that might be stuck in snow overnight and how comforting it would be to hear his voice. And for the hundredth time the thought that he believed her to be fickle and rude made tears start into her eyes and she had to make a real effort to control them.

Disaster struck soon after leaving Darlington. First there was a "waiting for further information" message as the train slowed to a crawl, then after getting going again they suddenly stopped completely and were told that the wind had changed, the snowstorm was intensifying and coming their way, and further information would be broadcast as soon as it was on hand.

The woman across the aisle from Amy leaned across and held up her phone. 'Have a look at this!' She put the phone into Amy's hand and watched her read the weather warning: Severe wind, extremely low temperatures and additional heavy snow forecast for northeast England. They looked at each other and shook their heads at the same time. No words were necessary because this was clearly going to be one of those occasions when a train was stuck for hours possibly getting colder and colder by the minute and without any food available, or perhaps an evacuation to somewhere to stay the night. After what seemed quite a long wait they were told that buses would be waiting on the road which ran alongside the railway track and each carriage would be evacuated in turn. Passengers were encouraged to be patient and wait until they were told it was their turn to leave, but to have coats and hats ready.

An hour and a half later Amy stood in the door with her overnight bag in one hand and her computer case slung over her shoulder, grabbed the hand of the man standing in knee deep snow and jumped. Snowflakes swirled on strong gusts of wind, and it was hard to see even an arm's length ahead. She ducked her head, pulled her beanie down more securely with one hand and tried to step in the footprints leading to what was presumably the road, but soon realised she was safer just looking ahead instead of at the ground, even if she could see very little. It was very dark, and the sloping ground was treacherous. A few metres from the train the light from the windows was obliterated. Just when Amy decided she must have lost track of where she was going and was lost, there was the road, and a bit further down to the right she could just make up headlamps through the snow blowing nearly horizontally. Behind her a woman's voice said, 'Oh, no! Oh, no!' which only served to make her walk faster, as if missing a step now might make the minibus she could just see though the swirling snow disappear. They and Thomas were the last to enter through the side door and as soon as they were seated the door was shut be someone on the outside. The woman who earlier had held out her phone in the train was in the seat in front of Amy, so she leaned forward to talk to her, but neither of them had any idea of exactly where they were.

'Do you think they'll take us back to Darlington? It can't be that far away, but it's hard to judge with all the stopping and starting we've been doing.'

Amy never got to reply because the driver twisted in his seat to talk to them. 'We're the last transport, the first bus headed back to Darlington, and I don't know where the second on went. But now the road's fast becoming impassable, so I'll head for the pub just down the road. It's quite big, but even if you don't get a room you'll at least be warm and safe. I don't think we'd make it back to Darlington and we don't want to be stuck in snow on the road overnight, so this is the safer option. I'll inform British Rail that's where I'm taking you.'

30

After a challenging drive through snow that had piled up in uneven drifts on the road they made it to the Swan and Badger Inn. The sight of brightly lit windows and lots of cars outside was a welcome break from gloomy thoughts and as soon as their driver slid the side door open they heard music even over the noise of the wind tearing through the trees along the parking lot.

Clutching their bags and holding on to headgear everyone made it to the front door as quickly as they could through gusts of gale force wind nearly desperate to get inside. Going through the door was like stepping into a different world, warm and bright with the sound of happy voices and laughter and loud music coming through closed double doors on the left. In the large entrance hall the last passengers from the previous minibus load were picking up their bags and disappearing up the stairs.

Amy's little group put their luggage down and shook snow off their jackets and, obedient to the instructions from the woman behind the desk, put their bags to one side by the stairs. Amy took the opportunity to go to the toilet and returned to find there was only one person ahead of her. When it was her turn she asked the cheerful but slightly stressed looking woman for a single room.

'Last one,' said the woman, whose name badge proclaimed her to be "Sally, Manager". She ran her pen over the entries in her ledger. 'It's called a single, but the bed is that size that used to be called "double" – slightly narrower than a queen size. It's the last room we have, number eight. Turn right at the top of the stairs and it's at the end of the corridor. It's got, its own bathroom with a shower, no bath. That will be one hundred and twenty quid with breakfast – provided we don't have a power cut. I'll give you a candle and a box of matches just in case, I've run out of emergency lanterns tonight. We often have power cuts here when there's a real storm – gales coming in from the North Sea can be destructive.'

She gave Amy a warm smile, her eyes glinting with amusement at the look on Amy's face. 'Don't look so worried! Plenty of warm quilts here, so you won't freeze in the night if the power and the heating go off. We're used to the odd day of snow and drama.'

As she turned to pick up the candlestick and box of matches already waiting on the desk behind her, steps approached from behind Amy, and she was enveloped in a strong smell of cinnamon. Sally looked past her and said, 'Did you already get a room, or have you just appeared?'

Behind Amy a familiar voice spoke. 'No, I've been in the bar having a beer while you processed the others. I'd like a single room please or whatever kind of room you can give me.'

'None left,' said Sally. 'Sorry! I'd offer you a sofa to sleep on in the lounge, but we've got a large group in there celebrating a fiftieth birthday and they're very likely to be stuck here for the night too unless they live really close - they've left it too late for most of them to get home, I think. Maybe you can find someone who will let you share their room. No single men to pair you up with, I'm afraid. One woman on her own has already gone upstairs, but ...' she paused significantly, 'I can give you a spare quilt to put on the floor to sleep on, though there are a couple of extra already in the camphor chest in this lady's room.'

She looked expectantly at Amy, patiently waiting for her to consider this solution.

Why on earth had Sally just suggested that two people, who as far as she knew were strangers, should share a room? If she hadn't been so confused Amy would have simply said, "No thanks" and headed upstairs, but she still hesitated. He hadn't realised it was her, she thought and still didn't speak, conflicted about what she should do. Keep her beanie on and just say "no thanks", take her key and leave him to his fate, or reveal who she was and see what happened next? As usual when she thought of him she was conflicted by the mix of emotions it generated in her, how much she wanted to be with him and how embarrassed she would be by what he obviously thought of her.

He'll probably gloat about Patrick marrying someone else after he thought I'd fallen in love with him. Or maybe he'll just treat me with disdain, because he must still think I just ghosted him when I fell for someone else. He won't know the other reason and I can't tell him. I'm kind of tangled up in my feelings about his inability to have compassion for those he writes about and how bad I feel about what I set in motion with that post to the Readers' Page. This is the worst thing that could have happened!

She had been silent for too long, and the manager was studying her face with concern, waiting for an answer. Then, without making a conscious decision, Amy pulled her beanie off and let her hair tumble out, turned around and found herself with nothing to say, bereft of speech exactly like Ben, who simply stared at her.

'I can see you two know each other,' said Sally with a slightly wicked grin that neither of them noticed. 'Maybe you can work it out between you. There aren't many options and any moment now the power could go off, and the folks in the lounge will start milling around dropping glasses on the floor and shouting for me to do something, so make up your minds! Here's the key, and the candle – the door's unlocked. I've got to go and be ready for the mayhem.'

She picked up a flashlight and disappeared through the swinging door behind her, and Ben cleared his throat but still said nothing, though Amy knew exactly what was going through his mind. He would have preferred to turn around and walk away, but there was nowhere to go, and he didn't want to plead, so he was waiting for her to say something.

She swung around, picked up the candle stick and the matchbox, slid her credit card back into her shoulder bag and took hold of her weekend case. 'Coming?'

Without a word Ben picked up his own bag, followed her up the stairs and they walked in silence along the passage to the room at the end. When Amy put her bag down to open the door she wondered if he would speak first, and what those words would be. Recriminations, scorn, anger?

Ben closed the door behind him, and they stood there in a spacious room with patterned carpet and a floral bedspread, neither of them taking in their surroundings, just looking silently into each other's eyes.

Then Ben pulled himself together with a visible effort. 'I'll obviously sleep on the floor,' he said abruptly and gestured to the space between the bed and the window. 'There's plenty of room, and I'll be fine sleeping on a quilt. And thank you for agreeing to share your room. I know you didn't want to.'

'That's OK.' Amy turned away, unable to meet his eyes for another second, while lust and embarrassment battled for supremacy in her mind. She looked more closely at the room and decided that the camphor chest at the end of the bed would be a good place to put her bag, but first she must get the extra bedding out. She opened the lid and threw two pillows on the bed, lifted out a quilt and a blanket and tossed them on the floor. 'Perfect!' she said and felt marginally happier. 'There's enough stuff here for you to make a comfortable bed for yourself.'

Still silent, Ben shoved his bag closer to the wall with his foot and bent to lay out the quilt folded double. After hesitating for a moment, Amy turned her back and opened her case to avoid having to talk to him. She grabbed what she needed out of her bag and retired to the bathroom feeling despondent at the thought of all that lay between them, the way she couldn't explain her actions and how uncomfortable it would be to lie awake in a dark room with him only a few feet away. It's fate punishing me, she thought gloomily, because I did it all wrong. I should have told him I was Julia Somerset and how he made me cry with his sarcastic comments, and how the only positive thing right then was that nobody knew that I'm Julia – how humiliated I felt. That would have been much better than what I actually did, and it's my fault we ended up like this with all these unspoken explanations and unanswered questions.

Staring at her own reflection while she cleaned her teeth, she couldn't think of a single thing she could say to Ben when she re-entered the bedroom, and decided the best plan was to simply slide into bed, close her eyes and pretend to go straight to sleep.

$\mathcal{A}$ few minutes later she came out of the bathroom in her sleeping T-shirt and panties, ready to hop straight into bed, and at the very moment she took a step into the room the lights went out. The room was suddenly completely dark, no ambient light came through the curtains from outside. The only sound was her own gasp of surprise and a little gurgling noise from the radiator under the window.

'Shit - where did I put the candle? Did you see where I put it?' Amy could hear that she sounded unreasonably upset, but being alone with Ben in a totally dark room was making her feel apprehensive. Having the candle lit would be a great improvement, at least until she was in bed.

His voice came from where he had put his quilt down by the window. 'I don't know, I didn't notice where you put it, but if you stand still where you are now, so I don't step on you, I'll try to find it.

'Maybe on the little table just opposite the bed,' said Amy. 'I think that's where I put the key.'

'No, not here.'

She heard him moving and imagined those large hands feeling for furniture corners, sliding carefully over surfaces and wished ... but no, she didn't wish that. That's ridiculous, so just stop it, she told herself. Try to control your wayward thoughts, you're acting like an idiot – well, you're thinking like an idiot. Just get a grip and control your mind.

Just then she realised that Ben was only a step away from her, she could feel his presence like a change in air pressure, and instead of taking a couple of steps forward towards the bed to get out of his way, she stayed where she was and waited.

Two seconds later his hand made contact with her left arm. He stopped moving and she held her breath, then they both said at the same time, 'I'm sorry!' But not in the tone of voice people use when they say a casual "sorry" to someone they have accidentally bumped into. This "I'm sorry!" was said with deep regret, as if they both genuinely apologised at exactly the same time.

His hand moved slowly up her bare arm and stopped at the curve of her shoulder, and she felt herself relax. That large, warm hand on her skin was so comforting and so welcome.

'What are you sorry about?' asked Ben as if genuinely wanted to know. 'For dumping me without a word?'

'It's complicated.' She paused, hesitated about

whether to continue and decided she had to. 'I wanted to punish you for being so insensitive and not understanding what I was trying to tell you. And for continuing to write hurtful things.'

'Well, you certainly did.' He didn't sound upset; he was just stating a fact. 'You did it very effectively. When the florist sent me an email and told me the flowers had been returned and the message on the envelope I knew I'd been gamed by a master planner.'

'Oh God!' said Amy feeling awful about herself. 'I didn't set out to trick you, I just wanted to make you see that your sarcastic humour was hurtful to many – to understand the difference between "group sarcasm" if I can call it that and naming and shaming an individual. And then ...'

'And then what?' His voice was still calm and casual, but she could feel the intensity behind the façade. He wanted her to explain in detail, to hear what kind of case she could put up in her own defence. And though it made her cringe inside she knew she must do it. But if she told him the whole thing, would she reveal a pathetic side and make herself look ridiculous? But she had to - this conversation couldn't end partway through.

'I fell in love with you, and I knew we had no future with such totally different outlooks, it would always be between us and ... it broke my heart. I'm sorry I didn't explain it, but I couldn't, I was too hurt.'

There was a long silence, but to her surprise his

hand remained warm and steady on her shoulder, and she didn't move by so much as an inch in case he realised and pulled it away.

'Are we friends?' asked Ben hesitantly. 'Enough so we can talk?'

She nodded in the dark, then realised that he couldn't see her nod. 'Of course we can talk. I've been wanting to talk to you for ages. I shouldn't have been … but it wasn't all … I mean…' There she stopped unsure of how to continue, for once in her life without words to express what she wanted to say.

There was another long silence, but his hand remained on her shoulder, and he ever so slightly increased the pressure of his fingers, and the feeling of that firm grip suddenly snapped her out of her mental deadlock.

'What I was trying to say was that after I cut you off, I missed you, a lot. I knew I'd behaved badly, but I couldn't cope. I've never felt so sad in my life. To give up what I really wanted was hard.'

'But you did and without telling me why. At first I thought it was …'

'I know what you thought! I'm sorry!' Her voice broke and she knew if she tried to continue speaking she would cry.

His hand moved over her shoulder blade and his fingers slid up through her hair and cupped the back of her head in that wonderful way he had done so many times before.

'I missed you so much.' His voice was hoarse,

and she knew he was telling the truth. He wasn't just taking advantage of her vulnerability and the situation they were in; he really had missed her instead of hating her for being cruel.

'Come here,' he said after another few moments of silence and pulled her against his chest, and she leaned into him with a sigh. She felt his warm breath as put his cheek against the top of her head, then his chest vibrated with that familiar chuckle. 'Who would have thought! Isn't this incredible? The two of us in this situation and one room left. It's like fate planned this storm just for us. But listen, and this is the truth – I've never stopped loving you, not for a moment.'

'Me too – my heart broke, it really did, and it was my own fault. I should have done things differently.'

He let go of her and took a step back, and she heard him sliding out or various articles of clothing, things dropped to the floor, his shoes kicked aside. There was a whoosh of air as he flung the bedspread aside and then - there he was. Large and warm and solid, just like she remembered, the only man she'd ever known who could inspire rampant lust and a sense of safety and comfort at the same time. She slid her arms around him, and he lifted her slightly off the floor and tipped them both sideways onto the bed. In what seemed like seconds he had stripped her T-shirt off and then his hands were on her body and there was no need for words. Some considerable time later, with the quilt thrown aside and the room getting colder by the minute, she lay curled against Ben's side, warm on the front and freezing cold at the back.

'God, I've missed you! I don't want to move, but we need that quilt back.'

Once they were covered up again, their combined body heat created a capsule of warmth under the covers, and Amy put her hand on his cheek and rean her fingernails over the stubble.

' I hope you'll tell me who Julia is,' said Ben drowsily after a few minutes and ran his hand down her side. 'It's obviously somebody you know - somebody you're fond of and that's why you decided to punish me. I'd like to tell her in person that I realise I was out of order – I want to apologise for how I must have made her feel.'

Amy nearly laughed. He knew that her comment on the Reader's page referred to Julia and he had worked out that she had written it, but he hadn't guessed that she herself was Julia.

'I'm Julia,' she said and tapped her forefinger on his cheek. 'I wrote those books.'

There wasn't long silence. 'Christ! That never occurred to me. Oh darling, I'm sorry! You must have felt so hurt.'

'I did,' she said, unable to keep humiliation out of her voice even now. 'It made me cry. I felt belittled and ridiculed, and my only comfort was that I'd never told a single soul that I was writing romantic novels under a pen name, so nobody could gossip about me and pretend to commiserate. I think that saved my sanity. Being anonymous enabled me to act normally when all I wanted to do most of the time was crawl into a corner and cry or kick someone to death – preferably you.'

'But you read my regret column, the one two weeks after you returned the flowers, didn't you?' Now he sounded nearly desperate. 'You didn't? Oh, shit! When I worked out what it was all about, which of course I did after I read that comment piece of yours on the Readers' page – and I knew it was you the moment I read it - then I assumed that Julia was someone close to you. All I wrote after that, bit by bit in one column after another, were things I was really telling you, hoping you were reading them.' He sighed. 'And of course, also telling my readership that I had changed, that someone had taught me a lesson.'

'I didn't feel like reading more of your columns,' said Amy and ran her forefinger over his eyebrow. 'I'd had enough of you for the time being, and I was so desperately unhappy about having let you go. I had to stop writing in the middle of a book because the fun had gone out of it, and I've only just recently started again, but it's uphill work being creative when you're deeply unhappy. I'm back in writing mode now, but only now and then.'

He pulled her closer, wrapped his arms round her and held her tight. 'Please read what I wrote!' His voice was a half growl, he sounded desperate. '*Promise* me you'll read those columns – because I wrote it all for you. I bared my soul in public, admitted I had gone too far many, many times and how I'd been made to realise how cruel my writing was at times. Apart from your name every detail is there, including the story about the returned flowers.'

She kissed the side of his neck, the part of him closest to her mouth. 'Thank you - I *will* read them.'

32

The scene that met Amy's eyes when she pulled the curtains back the next morning was such a contrast to the previous evening that she laughed out loud. 'Oh my God! We're on another planet – come and have a look!'

Ben came up behind her, pulled her back against his chest and kissed the top of her head. In front of them early sunshine lit a landscape still covered in snow, but today there was no wind, and the reflected light seemed to make the world glisten. From around the corner two cars appeared, turned onto the main road and disappeared at speed.

'All those people who were at the party will be keen to get home,' said Ben. 'I wonder if they slept on the floor – what a dramatic birthday party they had. And look at how fast the snow's melting on the road – it must be a lot warmer this morning.'

A knock on the door was followed by a man's

voice. 'I can hear you're awake. Breakfast in half an hour before the bus arrives to take you to York. Please bring your bags when you come down for breakfast.'

They took turns showering after Amy rejected Ben's offer of a shared shower. 'No thanks! The thought of being squashed against the wall of that tiny cubicle every time you moved – you're far too big to share a shower with unless it's one of those walk-in ones.' She reached up and kissed his chin. 'Not that I don't love the idea of having a shower with you, but not here!'

'Very smooth operation,' said Ben appreciatively once they were seated side by side on the bus. 'I texted my mum last night from the train and said not to panic if she heard about it on the news, pretended I was already evacuated. If I hadn't she would have called every half hour to check if I was ok.'

Shaking her head at how last night's drama and passion had knocked all normal conversation out of her mind, Amy smiled. 'Good grief, I didn't even think to ask where you've been.'

'Visiting my mother in Hexham. She's just had surgery on her wrist after a fall, so I thought I'd pop up and check she's doing alright and spend a couple of days. And then I did a little detour and spent half a day with a cousin I haven't seen for ages, years actually.'

'Where on earth is Hexham? I've never heard of it.'

'Halfway between Newcastle and Carlisle – it's where I grew up. And where have you been? I was as muddled as you were last night, didn't even think of asking why you were on the train.'

'Doing some financial detective work for a company in Newcastle. Will I see you in London or have you had enough of me now?'

He reached out and gripped hers tight. 'Don't even joke about it - I want to see you every day for the rest of my life. And you can take that look off your face. I'm not being funny or sarcastic, I'm serious. But you know that, right? You realise how special this is – that we met again by chance and were forced to share a room? It's like fate intervened and saved us.' He looked seriously at her. 'You can't imagine how surprised I was when you took your beanie off and all that spectacular hair tumbled out. Speechless!'

Amy smiled affectionately at him and said, 'I was only joking, Ben. Of course I know you want to see me – and I want to see you every day for the rest of my life too. I can't even describe what went through my mind when I realised you were coming up behind me. All my guilty feelings about how I treated you, and all my grief about what you must think of me after seeing that photo of me kissing Patrick. I'm surprised I didn't have a complete panic attack.'

He smiled. 'And instead, you marched off

towards the stairs and threw that brief invitation over your shoulder, as if it was of no importance whether I followed you or not. Epic!'

'Just like one of those romance novels you so despise – passion and drama, misunderstandings and resolution, and then that unlikely and unrealistic happy ending! Remember that?'

'Please, let's never mention it again,' said Ben and tightened his grip on her hand. 'I've totally revised my ideas about romance novels already. Feel free to use our story in your next book – it's got everything, all the right ingredients. You can dedicate it to me, and I'll write it up in my column, I promise. But one thing, though – what happened with the stunningly handsome Patrick? I thought you had fallen madly in love, both of you, and then he goes and marries someone else. Did he ditch you?'

Finally, thought Amy, the moment I so often wished I could somehow create to give me a chance to explain. 'No, no – it was never a love affair at all. It was part of a strategy to take the heat off him after some rumours that he was a closet gay – which his agents felt would be the worst thing for his career. Not the gay part, that wouldn't matter but how hiding it might make him seem dishonest and that might turn big companies off using him. Not to mention how sexy women find him, and if he was supposedly gay that would impact too. He actually met Kate through me – and the rest is history. I'll tell you the whole story soon, but not on a bus – it's the kind of stuff you could write a whole column about. And you'll obviously meet Kate and Patrick – they're both lovely and such fun.'

33

Getting back to London after all that had happened on the way back from Newcastle was like entering another reality. This feeling of time and place dislocation seemed to strike both Amy and Ben to the same degree and made them feel uncertain. When Ben said, 'I suppose I'll see you tonight, but ...' Amy said, 'Yes, of course, and ...' She hesitated to be the one to say where they would see each other, as if they had just met and weren't certain of each other.

But after a moment Ben laughed out loud and pulled her into a hug. 'Are we a couple or aren't we? Your place or mine?' and she laughed too, relieved that this strange episode had been resolved. 'Mine! You know where it is, and I haven't a clue where you live, and you like my views better than yours. I should be home by six, I hope.'

· · ·

Stefan was standing beside the reception desk when Amy walked in, and she pointed her finger at him and laughed. 'You have *no* idea what a good old blizzard coming in from the North Sea is like, do you? I seem to remember you don't believe blizzards actually happen, so let me tell you what it's like. It's like being an Arctic explorer. You jump down from a train into knee-deep snow in nowhere-land, there's a freezing, gale force wind blowing snow horizontally, and you can't see your hand in front of your face. Then you tramp through deep snow in total darkness and hope you're going to end up on the road, which you can't see, where a bus is supposed to be waiting. Terrifying – I should have flown.'

'But you were the one who said on no account would you fly unless the weather was perfect, if I remember rightly. But I'm sorry you had such a dreadful trip! I heard about it on the TV news last night and I wasn't sure what I could do. I didn't even know when you were due back, I was just checking with George now.'

'He sounds calm now,' said George, 'but before you walked in he was pretty worried – as was I. There's a lot of confusion on the British Rail website about where people ended up after several trains got stuck in the middle of nowhere. Where were you?'

Amy dropped her overnight bag and the laptop satchel on the floor and took her coat off. 'I spent the night at the Swan and Badger Inn in a place whose name I don't know, and I had a lovely time, thanks, once we got out of the blizzard. Oh, wait! We also had a power cut that lasted a few hours, but it was a great night.'

Stefan looked from her to George and back again and then they were all laughing. George gave her one of his deliberately naughty looks and said, 'I'm glad you had a great night!'

Stefan picked up her bags and led the way to her office, where he sat down in her visitor's chair and gave her a look of obvious speculation. 'I thought we'd better get away from that public area before the rest of them came out to check what all the laughing was about. A great night? What have you been up to? You look like that cat that got the cream.'

'My life is back on track,' said Amy seriously. 'I know you've been concerned about my strange moods, but it's all back to normal now. The most incredible coincidence you've ever heard of snapped me out of my misery, and I'm happier than I've ever been! I might even tell you all about it one day, but not right now. First I must tell you how it went in Newcastle.'

By mid-afternoon the report was finished, the details about dates and amounts, fake creditors and whose logon had been used for each transaction had been double checked, and Amy sat back after reading through it one last time, cross checking against her notes. She picked up her phone and sent a text message to Jordan to say the report would be sent directly to his email account within the next few minutes and would he please share it with Sonia before letting their auditors and the police see it.

'I think she deserves to be one of the first to read it after you,' said Amy when Jordan called straight back. 'She'd been neurotic about the situation for some time, but I don't know if she's told you about it yet. She knew that somehow money was disappearing, but she couldn't tack down how it was done or where it went, so she worried she would be suspected of doing it. She didn't think it was you, but she knew as well as we do that the nicest seeming people can be dishonest, or violent, for example, so she was trying to work it out on her own before she discussed it with anyone.

'No, I didn't know that, but of course I'll forward it to her,' said Jordan. 'And then to the cops, right after that. I met with our solicitor this morning and he'll start working on it the moment he gets your report, he'll liaise with the police. I can't thank you enough, marvellous work!'

Amy had no sooner put the phone down than George walked in with a mug of coffee and a pastry on a plate. 'You didn't get any lunch, so I got this for you from the café downstairs. I gather your mission went well?' Curiosity hung like a luminous mist around him and made Amy laugh. 'It went very well, I'm back to normal again – just telling you before you ask – and the job in Newcastle went well too, everything is sorted out and everyone's happy. Apart from the thief, of course.'

'I don't suppose you would ...'

'No, George, I would *not*! This needs to be kept under wraps for some time now, but let's just say that someone will be very sorry in the near future.'

Towards the end of the afternoon, after spending an hour with Grant, discussing a new job that had come in while she was away, Amy picked up her phone and realised she had muted it by mistake and now she had several message alerts.

The first was from Charlotte: *Just to tell you next instalment. Breannah and I met again, less wine this time but lots of fun, she's broken off with R and I've taken a solemn oath not to be tempted to let him back in my life. As if I would!*

Amy replied: *That sounds great, can't wait to meet her.*

Then a message from Pete: *Roger's making a tagine tonight, want to come for dinner?*

And a text from Ben: *Want to go out for dinner or eat at home?*

Amy replied: *I've been invited to Peter and Roger's for dinner, let's go together without telling them in advance.*

Reply to Pete: *I'd love to! Is half past seven OK?*

. . .

When Pete opened the door that night and saw Amy and Ben together he grinned. 'Wow, cinnamon man and no tears! Come on in – lovely to see you two are together again.'

The look on Ben's face made Amy realise that he was the only key person left now, who had never heard about the scent signature phenomenon, and the look of confusion on his face was comical.

'Cinnamon man? What's that supposed to mean?'

'Oh shit! Doesn't he know? You haven't told him yet?'

Roger appeared from the kitchen and looked at the three of them with an expression of disbelief. 'You lot talk exclusively in questions now? Is it a new trend? Am I missing out on something? Can I join in?'

Ben, who had looked searchingly at Pete, turned to Amy. 'Let's sit down somewhere and get this thing out of the way because I'm totally baffled. Why am I being referred to as "cinnamon man"? Is this one of your wicked tease-jokes?'

'It's how I knew you were there behind me in the line at the Swan and Badger – I smelt cinnamon, so I knew it was you.' She looked blandly at him and waited while he studied her face for clues, and Pete and Roger stood by, both smiling. Roger caved first and took pity on Ben. 'She's got this magic thing going, mate. And it's true, we both totally believe it.

Your signature scent is cinnamon, Pete's is lemon grass, and I don't have one, but she says it might develop over time.'

'Oh God! Are we going to have to go through the whole thing again?' asked Amy. 'Please give me a glass of wine first. Maybe we should try the one of the two I brought - I got them specially to try with the tagine. And you guys can tell him the story, I'm sick of it.'

On the way home very late that night, Ben was unusually silent, and Amy felt a tinge of worry. Maybe he had only pretended to believe the scent explanation and was going to dig in and try to find out why she had made up something so crazy, ask how she got Pete and Roger to believe it. But he noticed her expression and smiled. 'Are you worried about something? It's not the cinnamon thing, is it? I like being the cinnamon man.'

'So you believe it? You don't think I made it up?'

'Of course, I believe it. That story about the hot cooking oil and the man on the train that Pete told me – crazy! And how you knew your ex was in the Gamble room that time and you had to explain to Kate. As Pete said, it's like a science fiction novel, but clearly true - you're either a good fairy or a witch.'

inner with Patrick and Kate a couple of weeks later was an eye-opener for everyone. Once again a dinner invitation gave Amy the opportunity to show instead of tell that she was in a relationship.

'*Can you come for dinner on Thursday?*' texted Kate one evening, and Amy replied, '*Love to. Tell me the address please, I've never been to P's flat. May I bring someone?*'

'Perfect!' She looked at Ben who was standing by the window looking out over the canal and wondered if he was listening. The way he worked was fascinating and she was gradually getting used to these short periods of intense thought, when he heard or noticed nothing. 'We're having dinner with Patrick and Kate on Thursday.'

A few minutes later he turned. 'Did you say something?'

'We're going out for a surprise dinner on

Thursday. Secret location.' She wondered if her first comment when he was in his distracted bubble of concentration would come back to him later. After only a couple of weeks living together she still hadn't quite worked out the little quirks of his intense absorption in his work, particularly when he was writing the political column.

'Here we are,' said Amy on the Thursday night, after a short walk from the bus stop. 'This is the place, flat 8 is what we want.' She ignored Ben's nearly half-spoken question and pressed the button on the panel. The door clicked and she pushed it open. 'Come on!'

'Welcome!' said Patrick when they emerged from the lift. He was standing in the open door to the apartment, tall and as impossibly handsome as always, with a big smile on his face. 'Come in and we'll do the introductions. Kate's cooking something mysterious that needs her to stand beside the stove for the next ten minutes – come into the kitchen.'

This is hilarious, thought Amy five minutes later, sitting on the far side of a breakfast counter with a glass of wine in her hand. These guys have never met before, but the various connections! And they haven't discovered yet, they just know each other's names.

'Hey!' she said. 'Listen.- I think we need to map out how we all interlink and also why.' She pointed at each person as she spoke. 'Kate and I were introduced by Melissa and meet now and then at the Gamble room, and that's where she first discovered I can pick up what we call a smell signature from some men. Kate told me about the Ben_son column which I'd never heard of. So I went home and read a few from the online archive and discovered he had written a very harsh column about me. Not in his syndicated political column, of course, but in the other one, the so-called fun column.'

'Hang on! I'll explain, no questions, please! I write romantic novels under another name, but more about that later – he wrote a scathing thing about a book of mine that he used as an example. It made me cry.'

She drank some of her wine while three pairs of eyes were riveted on her face. 'And I met Patrick at my cousin Melissa's place and instantly liked him – his smell is freshly made coffee.' She took another sip of wine and decided where to go from here. 'Then I met Ben at my friend Pete's place – Ben's smell is cinnamon, which is also a favourite of mine. Kate asked me to join her and her friends for lunch once and they discussed your column, Ben, and that's when I made the connection and understood that you are Ben_son, the name of the fun column. So there's a whole lot of little coincidental facts.' She took another sip of wine and continued. 'And I then I fell in love with Ben and tried to get him to tone down the sarcasm in his column, and failed, and then Patrick asked me for help to stop rumours he was a closet gay. And from there everything went haywire – I ghosted Ben, he thought that famous public kiss with Patrick was for real, I cried when I couldn't explain to Kate why I was so sad, Patrick met Kate through me and now they're married! And finally, to close the circle, months later Ben and I were on the same train that got stuck in a blizzard and we had to share the last room in a pub *and* there was a blackout – and the rest is history. Clear as mud? Good!'

Now the others were laughing and talking over each other while Amy watched and listened and marvelled at how her life had turned around and how happy she was now. She snapped out of her thoughts when Ben clapped a hand on Patrick's shoulder and said, mock-threatening, 'And don't you *ever* kiss Amy in that passionate way again!'

'It wasn't me, truly – she assaulted *me*. Perfect move and perfect place to do it, though. She's a quick thinker.'

'You must introduce me to your father – I need to meet him, and I want to see his shop,' said Ben on the way home.

'What do you mean you need to meet him? Is there something about me you want to find out?'

'I just think he sounds amazing. You told me how he knew you were the result of an affair, and he just accepted it and never said anything about it – he's obviously an unusual man.'

'OK, we'll go on Saturday. We might need to

have a party, there are lots of people I want you to meet. How big is your flat?'

'Huge, and it's not a flat, it's a loft up under the roof.' He saw her look and grinned. 'Not like an attic! It's a massive, long room with four big skylights in the ceiling. Someone converted it before I bought it, and they did a great job. That big room, two reasonable sized bedrooms and a bathroom – with a tiled walk-in shower. I think I told you it's not got any views worth having, but it's full of light. At night I can lie in my bed and look up at the stars. We'll go for a visit in the weekend.'

That night Amy woke after a strange dream about Charlotte and Kirsten sitting at an outside café table at Coal Drop yard with an unknown woman and Frank, who was wearing a straw hat and sunglasses.

'Ben, wake up!' She poked him in the ribs, and he sat up like a jack-in-the-box. 'What? What's wrong?'

'Nothing, I just had a mad dream, sorry!' She told him about the dream and instead of striking him as concerning or possibly meaningful it made him laugh. 'It's that party idea of yours,' he said and pulled her close. 'Your mind is making up a guest list – let's talk about it in the morning.'

'Here it is.' It was Saturday morning and bright sun for a change, and they were visiting her father. Amy stopped outside the antique shop window and gestured at the display. 'This is the kind of things he sells. Antique furniture, silver and books.'

'Serious stuff!' Ben's eyes roved over the items in the window: a Georgian sideboard flanked by two Hepplewhite dining chairs, a silver jug and two goblets on the sideboard. 'Simple display, very impressive.'

'Those chairs are bound to be part of a set of six or eight,' said Amy. 'There might be table to match too. He rarely buys just a couple of anything – these are a teaser. He does make a lot of sales on the spot, he's very well known. And he has a huge following online and he posts images of things on his website. He also emails special customers if he finds things he knows they're looking for.'

'I must check the website.' Ben squinted up at the sign suspended outside the door. 'Somerset Antiques - the same as your pen name. Tell me why.'

'It was my mother's maiden name. Let's go in.'

The shop smelt of bee's wax polish and lavender, a smell Amy would always associate with her father, a smell that made her instantly feel that she had come home. They stood for a moment just inside the door and she could sense Ben's surprise at the how big the space was. 'Small on the outside and huge on the inside – like the Tardis.' She smiled. 'The building is narrow but very deep. Oh, hi dad! This is Ben.'

'Pleased to meet you! I saw you through the window, so I turned the coffee machine on.'

'Coffee machine?' Amy shook her head. 'Really? You bought a coffee machine?'

'Had it given to me, actually,' said her dad and led the way through the shop. 'Andrew, my neighbour, got it and he couldn't stand the hissing noise it makes, so he brought it in and said, "use it or sell it, I don't care". I like the coffee it makes. And we can't go out for lunch, so you'll have to go and get some stuff from the bistro down the road. A couple from Kent are making a special trip to check out the Hepplewhite suite, so I can't close for half an hour, or I might miss them. You saw the chairs in the window?'

'Part of a set, I bet. How big?'

'Eight chairs and a table long enough for twelve, plus a console table – and in great shape. I got them last month at an estate auction in a grand on old house just outside Bath.'

At midafternoon the couple from Kent turned up and despite Amy trying to leave quietly, Ben resisted and stayed in the background pretending to inspect Georgian silver while he listened. 'I had to,' he said when she finally got him out the door. 'I had a feeling it would be interesting to hear the conversation, and it was. He's such an authority on the things he sells, fascinating man! Would you like to inspect my loft now?'

'Oh my God!' Amy stood mesmerised just inside the door. 'It's gigantic! Just this room is as big as most two-bedroom flats. What a fabulous room! And look – it *has* got windows in the wall too.'

The long wall facing her had four long, windows quite high up, and she walked across to stand on tiptoes to look out. 'Ah, yes – I can see what you meant when you said you have no view. Never mind, it's another source of daylight. Show me the rest!'

Four weeks later Amy stood beside the long folding table they had bought the previous day. It was laden with food and drink, and she was mentally checking that everything was in place for the party they had planned in intricate detail for more than a fortnight.

'So many details,' groaned Ben. 'Can't we just buy a lot of wine and order in some food and hope for the best?'

'No, we can't – sorry!' Amy stuck her forefinger into Ben's chest. 'I have been to so many fabulous parties at Melissa's, and at Pete's place, and Patrick took me out for a dozen top class meals in expensive places, Charlotte is one of my very best friends and Kirsten is my little pretend-sister – I want to do this properly. Most of these people haven't met each other yet, so it's very special – not to mention they're getting to meet you!'

The invitations had gone out three weeks earlier

when they had decided to live in Ben's flat and give up the lease on Amy's. 'I want to make sure everyone can come,' she had said to her dad. 'I'm not a natural party-giver, so it's not going to be repeated any time soon.'

By half past seven the big room was buzzing with noise and laughter, and Amy was introducing people and talking, but her eyes were on the open door. She didn't want to miss Kirsten and Jonathan arriving. She had attended Frank's funeral shortly after coming back from Newcastle, but she had stayed in the background knowing that her half-sister Delia resented her existence. But Kirsten had spotted Amy at the back of the church and come over to give her a hug when everyone left at the end of the service.

And then she saw Jonathan's crest of faded red hair over the top of people who had moved between her and the door, and she abandoned Melissa and Aidan who she had just introduced to Stefan. The moment Kirsten spotted her she came up for a hug, and with her arm over Kirsten's shoulder Amy made her way through the crowd to the long table.

'Let's just stand just here side by side,' she said to Kirsten, the way they had planned it by text messages. She smiled at Jonathan. 'Let's see who notices first.'

And there they stood, very nearly the same height, their dark red hair in big lose curls over their shoulders contrasting with pale skin, both dressed in dark aubergine. Amy in her favourite dress and Kirsten in a top she had bought especially to wear with her white jeans at the party.

'Like sisters,' she whispered to Amy and giggled, while Jonathan, who had given his OK for this little performance, took a photo of them.

It only took a few minutes before the noise gradually died down as people turned to see what others were staring at. Amy's dad, who had been warned, had tears in his eyes and Ben looked as if he couldn't believe what he was seeing.

'Incredible!' said Melissa and burst out laughing. 'This is so funny! I thought you'd been cloned – you're just about identical.'

'Amy's just a little bit older,' said Kirsten cheekily. 'But otherwise we're just about the same.'

Hours later, leaving the mess for the morning, Ben peeled his shirt off and sat down on the edge of the bed. 'That scene was stunning – I just can't get over it. You and Kirsten, like twins born twenty years apart. She told me we should get a padlock with our initials and put in on the Millenium bridge because it's her favourite bridge in London.'

'No way! She's in for a disappointment if that's what she wants. I can't abide that stupid habit. Bridge rails that collapse and council staff spending ours cutting them off at great expense – ghastly habit.'

'We might have to – she thinks the train in the blizzard meeting is the most romantic thing she's ever heard of. She said a padlock would be perfect for us. Let me have a look at the big pad of yours with the guest list, so I can couple up the names with the faces while I remember them.'

Amy got into bed and passed over the pad that had lived on her bedside table for a couple of weeks while she made list after list with details for the party.

'Charlotte and Breannah, I talked to them for quite a while, Stefan – yep, that's your boss, and George I remember, very funny young chap. Who was Melissa's husband?'

'Aidan, the skinny guy with a moustache – mostly identified by how he brings golf and investment finance into social conversations.'

'Ah, yes – he nearly bored the pants off Rebecca. She told me she walked away right in the middle of a sentence after trying to change the subject a couple of times - she couldn't stand it any longer.'

Amy could well believe that. Ben's brother's wife was not a woman who put up with nonsense, but all she said was, 'Good for her – time someone did that.'

There was a text message on Amy's phone just before they turned the light out: *Don't know if you heard this, but I've been nominated as a spare grandfather by Kirsten, who said she couldn't see why not when we all know what happened. What a great little girl! Dad* small parcel wrapped in gold paper was waiting on the kitchen bench when Amy got up to make their weekend breakfast to have in bed, a habit she had introduced as an incentive for Ben to stay in bed instead of getting up straight away to have a shower.

'It's a nice, friendly thing to do,' Amy had said when she explained why she was prepared to make breakfast and bring it back to the bedroom for them to have together. 'It's nice and cosy to sit side by side in bed reading the news or whatever, eating toast and drinking coffee and then possibly having sex amongst the crumbs.'

And Ben had smiled his lovely, crinkly smile. 'That's the best reason I've ever heard for staying in bed on a weekend morning - having sex amongst the crumbs. Who could resist it?'

Now Amy called out in the direction of the

bedroom. 'What's this box? Is it an early birthday present? Is it for me?'

'It's for us. Bring it in here with the breakfast, so I can watch you open it. It's not really a birthday present, just a funny little thing I thought of.'

'OK,' he said a few minutes later. 'Now you can open it - and you're welcome to laugh at me for being silly and sentimental. This is something we talked about once and we laughed and mocked people who do this kind of thing, but I had this great idea.'

Amy ripped the gold paper and opened the little box and gasped. 'A gold padlock! I didn't know there was such a thing.'

'There wasn't – not until I had this one gold plated.' Ben chuckled. 'It caused quite a stir at the place I took it to. They said it was the first padlock they'd ever been asked to gold plate.'

Amy shook her head in amazement. 'It's gorgeous, but please don't say you want to put it on a bridge rail. I thought we agreed it's a silly habit that costs the councils thousands to have them removed with bolt cutters - or the bridge falls down from the weight of them.'

'Oh no, it's not going on a bridge. I'll tell you later where I'm planning to put it. I've got a forever place all worked out, a place where no one will ever find it. Did you notice the initials?'

On the back of the padlock were their initials with a + between them. Amy put the padlock down and leaned over to kiss him. 'Right away when I first met you I knew you were a romantic at heart. I thought to myself, I bet he secretly reads romance novels in bed at night, racing to get to the romantic happy-ever-after ending and then he goes to sleep with a smile on his face.'

On the Sunday morning when Ben as usual went for an early run, Amy sat down to write the final chapter in her fifth romantic novel and thought how wonderful it was to be able to live in the same flat with Ben and never feel that she wanted to be alone. Ever since she was adult and had a great job and a flat of her own, she had resisted living with anyone or having them live with her, because she felt her peace of mind depended on having time alone in a quiet environment and preferably writing. It was the way she recharged her batteries after a day of demanding work, her little treat in the weekends. But now things had changed and somehow just a couple of hours here and there was enough to recharge her batteries. To her surprise she found that she could write with someone else in the flat, provided it was the right person. Ben would often sit opposite her at the table with his own laptop, researching and reading about financial and political things or writing one of his columns.

This morning, he had left unusually early, and Amy got up as soon as he had gone, had a shower and settled down to write. When Ben returned just before lunchtime he had a funny look on his face when he gave her a hug. 'Sorry, that took so long, but I've been on a bit of a mission. I'll show you in a minute.'

He wasn't in his running gear, which she hadn't noticed when he left, and she wondered what he'd been up to. There was something going on, some kind of secret and she could tell he was excited. 'Shall we have lunch first or the surprise first?'

He got his phone out and handed it to her. 'Sit down and play this and I'll make lunch while you do it. It takes a few minutes.'

Amy took the phone, put a finger on the arrow to start the video and watched in amazement the scene that played out before her. There was Ben's nephew Michael, usually referred to as Squid, standing on a lawn with Big Ben behind him. 'That's Parliament Square,' said Amy surprised. 'What on earth were you doing in Parliament Square with Squid?'

'Keep watching!' came Ben's voice from the kitchen and Amy watched as Squid turned and walked towards a tall plinth, where the phone was passed from Ben to Squid. Then followed a slightly wobbly view of the environment and Squid's arm, which had her puzzled for a moment, before she realised that Ben had hoisted Squid up high for him to be able to grab hold and climb up on the plinth. The view swung down to show Ben standing on the grass and smiling up at Squid then up to show the huge bronze legs of the statue he was standing beside.

'My God, it's Churchill! What on earth is he doing?'

There was no answer from the kitchen, just a chuckle. Next followed a squirming sequence and Amy held her breath when she realised that Squid was somehow clambering up Winston Churchill's bronze body, pulling himself up onto Winston's arm, the one holding the walking stick, and then up his arm and onto his shoulder. He must have one of those phone harnesses strapped to his chest, thought Amy, thank God he isn't climbing and holding the phone in one hand. Next a hand holding the gold padlock appeared in front of the lens and the padlock was slipped down in the crease between the lapel of Winston's bronze military greatcoat and his neck, then a close-up of the gold padlock tucked securely into the fold in the bronze. Suddenly the view went through a dizzying tumble as the phone was dropped down and apparently impressively caught by Ben before it hit the paving. Next a shot from a bit further back showing Squid squirming and sliding down Winston's body onto the plinth beside his leg, then hanging by his hands from the edge of the plinth and dropping to the ground.

'Christ!' exclaimed Amy and put the phone down. 'What an amazing performance, and that drop at the end - he could have broken his ankle.'

'We looked it up afterwards,' said Ben, who had appeared in the kitchen door. 'That plinth is about two and a half meters tall, and the statue is nearly four meters. Isn't the bit where he stands on Winston's arm amazing? And how he slides down Winston's body to get down again?'

Amy got up and stood on tiptoes to kiss Ben. 'You are amazing! What a fantastic place to put the padlock, and nobody else will ever know it's there. I hope you're not going to show his mom this. She'd have a heart attack – I nearly did.'

'Oh no,' said Ben calmly. 'She would forbid me to ever take him anywhere again, she'd be furious with us, well, mainly with me. Squid and I agreed this will be a secret between him and us two, and he'll never tell anyone that he planted a padlock inside Winston's coat. I told him the minute he did, someone would talk about it and then it would be stolen.' He chuckled. 'When he was a toddler he used to squirm and clamber up my legs and up my body without me helping him at all until he was sitting on my shoulders, and we used to say he was like a squid because he seemed to have multiple arms and suction cups. He climbed out of his cot in the middle of the night, right over the side when it was up, long before he could crawl, and then he'd be stuck sitting on the floor under the cot screaming for help.'

'I'm surprised you weren't arrested. Aren't there cops all around Westminster these days?'

'One did approach just after we'd finished.' Ben laughed. 'We got a real telling-off for Squid climbing on the statue, but in the end he just told us to go away and never do it again. Squid saved the day and said he'd asked me to film him doing it because he liked Churchill – the cop couldn't resist him.'

'Most people can't, he's a little charmer. Another couple of years and he'll have girls crawling over broken glass to get to him.'

'Let's have one of our own just like him,' said Ben casually. 'Or maybe two? What do you think?'

And Amy smiled because the subject of having a family had never been mentioned, but she had thought about it lately and hesitated to bring it up for some strange reason. 'Yes, let's,' she said now. 'But we'd better start working on it right away – I'm not getting any younger.'

Ben shook his head. 'Forever young – and totally gorgeous.'

THANK YOU

We hope you've enjoyed reading this story and would consider leaving a review, or even a rating.

These are not only much appreciated, they also help other readers discover new authors.

For other titles from Lightpool Publishing, please read on.

ABOUT SASKIA

Saskia Woodhill is an author of soft romance novels where slightly paranormal characters occasionally engage in outrageous behaviour and sometimes find themselves in funny or dangerous situations - or funny and dangerous at the same time. Stories that will make you laugh and cry and turn the pages to a satisfying ending.

Julia, owner of a successful garage and used to working with men, prides herself on her practical and down-to-earth nature. But her calm and orderly world is about to change forever.

After a concussion, she disturbingly starts hearing the thoughts of others as spoken words in her mind. First, it's her sister, then it's Milton, the sexy customer with the sarcastic smile, and the man Julia is irresistibly drawn to, despite his outrageous thoughts.

Available from all good bookshops

A timeslip story with a difference: a lonely widow, a man who came from nowhere, and a sensual, slow-burn romance.

When a naked stranger collapses through Abigail's front door on a snowy night, her usual caution deserts her. Instead of calling the police, she finds herself harbouring this mysterious man who claims to be from the future.

But not her future – a future in another dimension.

Despite her scepticism of anything paranormal—and her hard-learned wariness of men interested in her wealth—something about him breaks through all her defences.

Available from all good bookshops.

OTHER TITLES FROM LIGHTPOOL PUBLISHING

Letters from the Past by Tina Clough is a series of stand-alone novels where a letter from or about the past reveals something that changes a woman's perceptions of her family, and affects her outlook on life. Life can change in a moment and sometimes you have to step into the unknown and take a chance on love.

Having had nobody in her life since her husband died, Lara unexpectedly finds herself involved with three men. One is planning to use her, one she plans to use for her own ends, and one becomes a "friend-with-benefits" with surprising results. Sometimes a quiet schoolteacher is not all she seems at first glance.

Callista experiences an event of apparent ESP at the Okehampton Castle ruins and becomes a media sensation, but the effect it has on her life is dramatic. How do two people, one calm. one seriously claustrophobic, who feel they are poles apart, cope for an hour and a half in total darkness in a stalled lift? And can they handle the consequences?

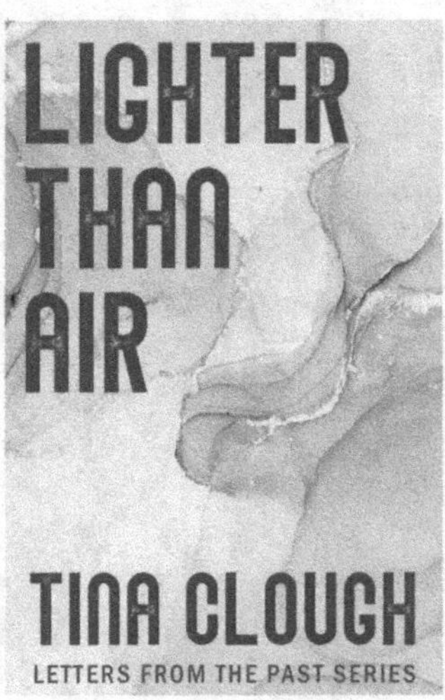

Sofia's life is in turmoil: a difficult diva mother, a letter with a confession about a family killing and having to accept help from a man she loathes when she is injured. Can reluctant attraction turn into love?

Who is the stranger living in the empty house Miranda inherited from her grandmother? Why is he living like a secretive recluse in someone else's house? Reckless Miranda decides to confront him, and what she discovers prompts her to set out on a fearless quest to bring justice to a man who has given up hope. But is the gamble too great or a risk worth taking?

When Emma finds an old letter in a library book she is instantly intrigued, but by researching the origin of the letter she unwittingly opens the door to danger and becomes the target for threats and harassment. Nearly desperate, she takes a leap of blind faith into the unknown and accepts an offer of help from a stranger - but can she trust him?

Jamie, an ardent protester against the gigantic Vista Resort development and Leo Masters, the high-powered developer, seem unlikely to ever agree on anything. But unexpected coincidences and chance brings them together in a fragile state of mutual respect. Will courage and kindness resolve the situation, or do they need help?

After a bizarre accident with ESP overtones, the media haunt Arapera. But can she trust an offer of help from a man she has only met once? Or will she regret it for the rest of her life if she doesn't take the chance? Sometimes life is a knife-edge balance between staying safe and taking risks, and there is no way of predicting if the gamble is worth it.

When crime-writer Saskia finds an unconscious stranger, she has a strange and strong emotional connection. Pretending to be his cousin and with no thought for the consequences, she spends weeks at his hospital bedside. But what will happen when he wakes and discovers she has invaded his life, breached his privacy and made crucial decisions on his behalf?

THE GIRL WHO LIVED TWICE

What would you do if you woke up one morning and found that time had rewound exactly a year? Would you revisit your past mistakes and try to do better? Would you try to get revenge on those who had wronged you? Or would you use what you knew to get rich? When Mia finds herself in her own past, she must decide how best to use her pre-knowledge of one year's worth of events and personal issues.